"I don't want thi

He had no problem telling her the truth. "I can't remember the last time I've had so much fun."

"Me, too, Kyle." She hung her head again, then glanced back up at him.

He felt it then. Something was happening between them. But he didn't know if Nikki felt it, too. Sure, he knew she had a crush on him before, but he figured by now she'd outgrown that. Moved on, especially in light of what happened.

He held out his hand for Nikki, hoping she'd take it. "Will you come over, then? Let me cook for you?"

A tender smile lifted the corners of her pinkish lips. Beautiful lips.

"I'd like that."

When Nikki placed her hand in his, his heart floated on a blanket of warmth. Soaring thousands of feet from the earth in a hot-air balloon had nothing on this.

Books by Elizabeth Goddard

Love Inspired Suspense

Freezing Point
Treacherous Skies
Riptide

Love Inspired Heartsong Presents

Love in the Air

ELIZABETH GODDARD

is a seventh-generation Texan who grew up in a small oil town in East Texas, surrounded by Christian family and friends. Becoming a writer of Christian fiction was a natural outcome of her love of reading, fueled by a strong faith.

Elizabeth attended the University of North Texas, where she received her degree in computer science. She spent the next seven years working in high-level sales for a software company located in Dallas, traveling throughout the United States and Canada as part of the job. At twenty-five, she finally met the man of her dreams and married him a few short weeks later. When she had her first child, she moved back to East Texas with her husband and daughter and worked for a pharmaceutical company. But then, more children came along and it was time to focus on family. Elizabeth loves that she gets to do her favorite things every day—read, write novels, stay at home with her four precious children and work with her adoring husband in ministry.

ELIZABETH GODDARD

Love in the Air

HEARTSONG
PRESENTS

Recycling programs
for this product may
not exist in your area.

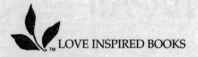

™ LOVE INSPIRED BOOKS

ISBN-13: 978-0-373-48674-8

LOVE IN THE AIR

www.LoveInspiredBooks.com

Printed in U.S.A.

But one thing I do: Forgetting what is behind and straining toward what is ahead, I press on toward the goal to win the prize for which God has called me heavenward in Christ Jesus.

—*Philippians* 3:13–14

Dedicated to: Jeff, Tina, Kristin and Aunt Elaine.

Acknowledgments

Every author has their team of experts to fill in
the holes where personal experience falls short.
Special thanks to Erin Thero of World Balloon for
her willingness to answer all my questions. She added
a heaping dose of warmth and friendliness to every
conversation. Thanks to my above-named family
members for their input. I enjoyed hearing about your
experiences and the wonders of the balloon world.

Chapter 1

The propane burner flared, torching the quiet dawn in the empty field.

Nikki Alexander never grew tired of the familiar sound she'd heard since childhood. After the fan blew enough cold morning air inside the rainbow-colored envelope to give it shape, she aimed the flames inside the balloon, which still rested on its side. Once the air began to heat, it would become lighter than the surrounding cooler air.

After a few minutes of hot-air bursts, the envelope lifted upright. "Lenny, stay with the basket and hold it down with me," she said.

The new kid on the crew, a local high-school student, worked in exchange for learning everything he could about balloons so he could eventually pilot his own. "Okay, boss!"

Nikki smiled and nodded at the freckle-faced kid. She figured anyone willing to get up before dawn to crew a balloon ride deserved the chance. Balloons were typically launched during the early-morning hours or late evening because the winds were lighter, making for easier takeoffs and landings, and she could avoid thermals—when the ground heated up and caused vertical air currents.

She'd already experienced difficulty in controlling her balloon on such an occasion, an experience she didn't want to repeat. Nor would her passengers appreciate a downdraft that could force the balloon into a hard landing—that and power lines were a balloon's greatest dangers. That was why even though some people requested more convenient ride hours, Nikki had to turn them down.

She glanced at the scene around her, making sure the rest of the three-man crew—David and Richard—were in position to keep the envelope from rising too soon. The field she typically used for launch was situated next to Sky High Rides, perfect for the winds from the west, which would urge the balloon slowly toward the east and several wide-open fields, where Nikki had arrangements with the landowners.

Her soon-to-be passengers—a man, his wife and their two children—stood back, all eyes wide with amazement, except for the teenage daughter, who focused on an electronic device, probably texting her boyfriend because she wasn't happy about having to get up before sunrise. Or she was angry because she'd had to leave him behind. The younger of the siblings, the boy, looked about seven or eight, which was her nephew Michael's age. Already, Nikki could see the light in his eyes and knew he'd never forget this experience. Often one ride was enough to turn someone into a lifelong enthusiast.

Nikki had grown up in the balloon-ride business. Her father, the founder of Sky High, had created a successful business before he died eight years ago. She'd begun her career on the balloon crew and eventually she'd learned to fly and gotten her balloon pilot's license. At twenty-eight, she had thousands of flight hours to her credit.

The balloon finally ready, she turned to the family and beckoned them forward. She'd already debriefed them on safety. Now they could climb into the basket.

Except that she spotted two familiar figures standing next to a white town car. Her mother stood behind Michael, gripping his shoulders as if holding him back.

"Richard, would you and Lenny mind assisting the family into the basket and wait for me." Nikki trotted over to the car, tension building at the base of her head.

"Mom, what are you doing here?" She crouched to eye level with Michael and hugged him.

"As soon as you left this morning, he started at me again, begging to go with you." Her silver-haired mother hadn't bothered to paint on her usual makeup this early in the morning and looked at least ten years older than usual. "Nikki, you've got enough room in the basket."

The Sky High baskets were commercial size. This particular basket could carry up to fifteen people, but Nikki shook her head anyway. "We've talked about this, Mom."

"Can I ride in the chase car?" Michael looked so much like Nikki's brother with his blue-gray eyes. He stared at her now, pleading just the way she'd seen Jordan do so many times growing up.

Her heart kinked at the reminder. None of them had recovered from losing Jordan in a balloon accident three years before, least of all Michael, who'd lost his father that day.

Although what happened to her brother was an unusual accident, flying still presented dangers, especially if the pilot was a risk-taker. Nikki would do everything in her power to send Michael on another path. She wouldn't stand by to watch him follow in his father's daredevil footsteps.

But right now, she could hardly fight the pleading she saw in her nephew's gaze, especially if her mother wasn't strong enough to keep from making the drive over.

She stood up. She'd have another talk with her mother about this later. "Michael can ride with David in the chase car this time."

"Yippee!" Michael threw his arms up and jumped in victory. He took off running, but Nikki snatched him back.

"Hold on there. I'll walk you over." Nikki spotted the family already waiting in the basket, and her crew at the ropes, keeping the balloon earthbound. Of course she'd need to heat the air inside even more to send it floating skyward.

Nikki buckled Michael into the van pulling the equipment trailer. David would drive the van and meet her at the agreed-upon location unless her landing coordinates changed. From there, they would load the equipment on the trailer and bring the family back to their vehicle.

Once she was inside the basket and her passengers prepared, she ignited the flame in the burner, heating the air. Her crew let go of the tether lines.

Slowly, the basket drifted upward.

Nikki looked down and waved at Michael, who watched her from the van. David, Richard and Lenny loaded the rest of the equipment on the trailer and prepared for the chase. She would soon become a tour guide, telling the family about the various sights they would encounter along the ride.

But for the moment, the group was held captive by the fact they were floating in the air, far above the earth.

"It feels like we're dangling here, not moving." Finally, the teenager's attention was stolen from her focus on texting.

Nikki smiled. "That's because we're drifting with the

current. You won't sense movement or even that we're very high, but of course, you can see that we are."

When the father took it upon himself to explain balloon flight to his children, Nikki allowed him the task. She held back when he got a few things wrong. By the smile on his face, he enjoyed impressing his kids, and she wouldn't ruin that for him. She allowed her thoughts to drift with the balloon, back to the girl's words.

It feels like we're dangling here, not moving.

Unfortunately, that was exactly how Nikki felt about her life these days. After her brother's tragic death while participating in the world's oldest balloon race, Nikki wanted to sell the family business, to move her little family, which consisted of Michael and her mother, far from the memories. And far from the reminders of the man she once loved.

But there always seemed to be something or someone standing in her way.

Kyle Morgan sat in Jordan's old office, staring at a stranger.

He tried to smile and keep calm while he answered Mark Zimmer's interview questions, but myriad memories lashed at his mind, distracting him. Mark hadn't worked at Sky High back when Kyle was here, and in fact, he looked as if he should be retired. Kyle figured that Nikki hired the man after her brother died. After Kyle had left the business, had left Albuquerque altogether, believing he would never return.

Guilt snaked through him—he'd left her in a difficult situation, which he was sure she hadn't forgotten. With that thought, he wasn't sure he hadn't made a mistake in coming here today.

Mark leaned forward and studied Kyle, yanking him from his tumultuous thoughts. The man assumed Kyle had stopped in to apply for a job as a balloon pilot, so he'd played along, because all things considered, this could be his best chance to see Nikki.

To get close to her again.

The timing couldn't be better—her business was in dire need. After Kyle presented his pilot license—both private and commercial—and discussed his experience piloting balloons while living in Texas, Mark made it sound as if Kyle was the only man for the job. Kyle left out that he'd once been part of the Sky High team in Albuquerque. Nikki must have wiped Kyle's memory from the place, eradicating photographs of him and Jordan with their balloons from the walls, because Mark didn't have a clue about Kyle's history here. Didn't the guy recognize his name as one of the participants in the Gordon Bennett with Nikki's brother? Maybe he hadn't been into ballooning very long.

He grinned at Mark as if he'd listened to everything he'd said about the business. But what could the new business manager—at least new to Kyle's way of thinking—know about Sky High that Kyle didn't already know? He'd practically grown up working in this business, working alongside his best friend, Jordan. Working alongside Jordan's sister, Nikki—that was, until that last race.

Mark leaned forward on the desk, drawing Kyle's focus back to his words. "The fiesta is just six weeks away, and we need someone who not only pilots balloons but can assist in other areas as the need arises. You seem to have a lot of experience under your belt, but what brings you to Albuquerque?"

Now, there's a loaded question.

He couldn't exactly tell the man that he'd intended to finally own up to his promise to Nikki's brother to watch over her and her brother's son, Michael. To help her with her business, because then he'd reveal just what a class act he'd really been to leave her in the first place. Nor could he tell Nikki what Jordan had asked of him as they both faced certain death together.

"This is where I'm from, and I just wanted to come home. I've missed New Mexico." His parents had died years ago, so it wasn't as if he had family to come back to, but no sense in bringing that up, or diving into the real reasons for his return. "I'm a contract programmer, so I can work anywhere I want. Set my own hours."

Perfect for being part of a balloon crew. At twenty thousand dollars and up, he'd never owned his own balloon anyway, so piloting balloons for others was his only way into the sky.

"How soon can you start?"

"You serious?" Kyle could hardly believe it was that easy.

"I needed you yesterday."

"Then I'm your man. How about immediately?"

Mark grinned and stood, made his way over to a filing cabinet and opened a drawer. Kyle allowed his smile to fall flat, letting down the veneer that was quickly wearing on him.

He'd made his share of mistakes, but he couldn't have known his need for daredevil thrills would end in the death of his best friend.

Did Nikki blame him for that? Would she even allow him to work here? She might think he'd gone about getting hired on in an underhanded way. If that was how she felt, she could easily solve the problem by showing him the door.

Mark set some papers in front of Kyle. "Fill this out if you want to get paid."

Then he left Kyle alone in the office. Half the wall was

glass from about three feet up, so Kyle could see into the warehouse from where he sat. Mark was on the phone and stood near a balloon basket pulled from the trailer where it had been stored. A large envelope in a brilliant rainbow of colors—red, yellow, green, purple—lay spread out over the floor.

Daydreamer... My old balloon.

His breath hitched. He hadn't noticed it before because he'd come into the office through another door, not through the warehouse.

Eager to get started, Kyle busied himself completing the employment paperwork, though maybe he should have gone about this in a different way, since he knew the owner personally. On the other hand, that thinking could be presumptuous.

After he finished filling out the forms, he left the office to give them to Mark.

Mark ended the call and took the papers. "First thing I need you to do is an inventory of the spare parts we have, and do a complete inspection of all the balloons. Make sure they're still in one piece. You're not the only pilot I need to hire. The fiesta is our busiest time of year, and it's our best chance to build the business back up to where it needs to be."

Kyle stared at the man. What was he missing?

"We've had some problems lately. Vandalism. Just some kids, probably. Tomorrow, we start taking on more rides. You know what that means, don't you?"

"Yep. I'll have to be an early riser to be in this business. What about my crew?"

"If you have people you know and trust—fine. If not, I have a few extras I can call. This one is yours. Check it out. Make sure it's safe." Mark gestured at *Daydreamer* splayed across the concrete floor.

When the phone in his office rang, Mark left Kyle to himself. It was difficult to watch the man pacing around in what used to be Jordan's office, so Kyle looked back at the balloon.

He crossed his arms and stared at the mass of fabric. Vandals, huh? He'd better make sure everything was in working order. He'd like Mark to give him a little more information about that, but it could wait.

Bending over, Kyle lifted a small section of the envelope, rubbing the balloon fabric between his fingers. He closed his eyes at the rush of memories—he'd left this behind just three years ago.

This balloon and much more.

A lump expanded in his throat. He dropped the fabric, dreading the moment when he would finally see Nikki. He feared her reaction, and yet he'd missed her, missed the life the three of them had shared. A life they could never get back.

What would she say when she saw him? Would she welcome him? And what would she say when she learned that he'd been approached by sponsors to enter the Gordon Bennett again, the world's oldest gas-balloon race—the same race that had left his best friend, her brother, dead?

A race he'd barely survived.

Would she understand that he had come back to keep his promise and to make amends to her while he still had the chance?

A noise drew his attention away from the balloon that he'd flown years ago while working for Sky High.

A dark-haired beauty stood frozen, staring at him from across the small warehouse. At the sight of her, his pulse rocketed.

"Nikki…" He took one step forward.

She took one step back.

Chapter 2

A full five seconds ticked by before Nikki registered that Kyle Morgan stood in front of her, and when it finally hit her, the realization sucked the oxygen from the building.

"What...what are you doing here?" Catching her breath, she gripped a nearby shelf to steady her trembling legs. Dust swarmed around her, reminding her that she was shorthanded.

A crease spread across his forehead when he took another step toward her. "Your manager just hired me."

Her heart hammered against her ribs. What had Mark been thinking to hire this man? Then again, Nikki had never told him anything about Kyle, preferring to erase him from her existence altogether. That had proved more impossible than she imagined, both emotionally—and now physically.

The balloon fiesta would begin soon, and she'd lost a pilot, leaving her as the lone rider, not to mention all the extra things required to run her late father's balloon business. A business he'd built up to the point that having the warehouse—an established physical location—made sense. And now…she could hardly stand to see how far things had fallen since the accident.

She hated that Kyle was here now to see that they were struggling, but he was partly to blame. Mark didn't know that.

To be fair, she'd given Mark the go-ahead to hire a pilot or two. And Kyle might be part of the solution, if Nikki could work with him.

She'd known that finding the right person wouldn't be easy considering that a good many balloonists were merely enthusiasts. If anything more than that, they could simply pilot their own clients. Who needed to work for Nikki?

But she'd never expected—not in a million years—to see Kyle again, much less working at Sky High.

"I haven't seen you in three years, not since…" She shouldn't have voiced her thoughts.

This didn't seem like the time to dredge up her brother's fatal accident. She'd never actually told Kyle she blamed him for Jordan's death, just figured he knew. She forced a smile, hoping it would hide the tumultuous emotions roiling inside.

Above her, the fluorescent lights flickered and buzzed, and one of them went out, leaving the far corner of the warehouse dark.

Kyle strode toward her, closing the distance between them until he stood only a few feet away. Not nearly far enough. Was it just her, or were his shoulders broader now? His thick black hair, rugged jawline and athletic physique had always taken her breath away. Since he'd been her brother's best friend growing up, she'd known him almost as well as Jordan. She'd considered him kindhearted, thoughtful and brilliant. He was every girl's dream. Nikki's dream until... She sighed, shoving those memories aside. They only clouded her thoughts.

But it was no use.

Despite all her pent-up resentment, her heart raced at the sight of him, just the way it used to. Still, Kyle had never returned her interest then, and so much stood between them now, so what was the point? Confusion corded around her throat.

"Look, I know it's a surprise to see me here." He squeezed the bridge of his nose, giving her the impression that seeing her pained him. "Honestly, I didn't come here looking for work."

"Then why did you come?" She hated her accusing tone. It left no doubt that she still felt something for this man, and she'd prefer not to let him know that he affected her either way.

"Is it so hard to believe that I wanted to see you?" Kyle stood closer now, his hazy blue eyes searching hers.

Not so long ago, she'd hoped to see a spark of romantic interest behind them. There was definitely something different about him now. Something different in the way he looked at her. If only she could sort through the chaos igniting in her head, in her heart.

"Yes. No," she said. "I don't know."

"How are you?" he asked.

The simple question was the sort of thing you'd hear from a casual acquaintance you happened upon in the grocery store. "Fine," she said.

"Let me ask that again. How are you? *Really?*" His gaze intense, he probed much deeper.

Nikki drew in a shaky breath, uncertain of her answer, even if she were willing to give one.

"Uncle Kyle!" Michael came running from the restroom and headed straight for Kyle.

Oh, great.

After their balloon ride this morning, she'd stopped here before dropping Michael off at home with her mother. He called Kyle his uncle because Kyle had spent so much time with their family before the accident and the name seemed appropriate. Kyle reached out and Michael jumped right into his arms, ecstatic with laughter. Nikki hadn't expected her nephew to remember Kyle so well, considering Michael had only been four when Kyle left them behind. Only four when he'd lost his father. The child couldn't remember his mother because he'd only been a year old when she left them, claiming she couldn't handle the responsibility of a child. How could anyone just leave like that?

And then there was Kyle.

What am I going to do? She'd hardly had time to digest Kyle's apparent attempt to step back into her life and evaluate whether or not she welcomed him. Michael didn't deserve more heartbreak—like growing attached to Uncle Kyle again only to have him disappear. She could blame Kyle Morgan for Jordan's death, but anything that happened to Michael, she had to blame on herself.

She'd need to have a serious talk with Kyle before she allowed him to remain here. The fact that she even considered the possibility of letting him stay scared her.

Mark stepped from the office and approached the small gathering. "I see you met the new guy, and by the looks of it, he's not so new to you."

"Hi, Mr. Zimmer," Michael said.

"Howdy." Mark directed the word to Michael but eyed Kyle.

Kyle squeezed Michael, love in his eyes, then put him down. "You've grown so big, little buddy."

"Don't call me that. I'm the sheriff." Michael flashed a huge grin. "Sheriff Michael."

"Sheriff Michael it is." Kyle put on a serious face, though amusement glimmered in his eyes.

Warmth flooded Nikki's heart. If he felt that way about Michael, then why had he left them? Why had he stayed away for so long? Where had he been the past three years? Michael could have used a father figure.

No. She was positive she didn't want to know where he'd been. Kyle wouldn't be a good role model anyway. He wasn't someone she or Michael could count on.

She schooled her features. "No, not so new. Kyle and my brother were close friends growing up. In fact, he used to work with us here at Sky High."

Mark wouldn't have known their history, or Kyle's accomplishments as a balloonist, because he'd come from the RV industry.

Though his eyes widened, he quickly recovered from his surprise. "Well, looks like he came back at the right time. Instead of turning people away, I've just booked us for the next few weeks. Business is back in full swing, and just in time for the fiesta, too."

Her business manager had simply overlooked the obvious question—why hadn't Kyle revealed his history? But Kyle was their best chance during a critical time. Miss this opportunity to book their schedule solid, build the business and restore the Sky High reputation, and they could forget about it until this time next year.

Mark knew that, as did Kyle.

Unfortunately, so did Nikki.

"Can you take me to get ice cream, Uncle Kyle?" Michael's question caught Kyle off guard.

Kyle hesitated, given the odd mixture of resentment and warmth spilling from Nikki's eyes—an unusual, striking blue shade that reminded him of warm blueberry pie. He knew he'd missed Nikki and Michael but only now realized just how much.

"Uncle Kyle has some work to do first." Nikki took Michael's hand and held on. "And I need to get what I came for then drop you off at home."

Did that mean that Nikki would let him stay? The tight clamp on his chest eased. For a few minutes there, he thought she was going to kick him to the moon for showing his face. They had plenty of unfinished business between them. His fault. But he didn't doubt she would give him the full force of her opinion when the time came. That was part of why he was back, wasn't it? To tell her how sorry he was. To make amends.

He doubted he'd get that chance after he told her he'd entered the Gordon Bennett. Helping her get the business through this rough spot was the least he could do, so he'd keep that news to himself for a little longer.

"Please? Uncle Kyle used to take me to get ice cream all the time." A glimmer in his eyes, Michael put on his best pouty face. "Besides, it's Saturday, and Grandma is boring."

Kyle jumped in before Nikki could give a firm no. "Let me finish what I have to do here, considering it's my first day on the job. I'll stop by later to get you, and we'll go get ice cream—that is, if Nikki says it's okay."

Nikki's hesitation gave Kyle courage to push forward. "All three of us can go."

He grinned at Nikki, hoping to disarm her. Convince her to give him a chance.

By the look in her eyes, Kyle knew that Nikki couldn't resist Michael, even if it meant getting ice cream with an unwelcome reminder from her past.

Battling a frown, she smiled in the end. "I have errands

to run this afternoon, but I guess that would be all right. After supper, then?"

"I'll stop by around six-thirty." He studied her, hoping to see a hint she had warmed to the idea that he was back. That he was here.

A warm sensation swirled inside his stomach. Unfamiliar ground where Nikki was concerned. As his best friend's sister, she'd been off-limits per Jordan's request, and Kyle had never thought of her as anything other than a friend because of that, though he'd suspected that Nikki liked him. Funny that Jordan, though gone now, still stood between them, but for many more reasons than before.

Mark cleared his throat. The look he gave the two of them made Kyle wonder if the man read something between Nikki and Kyle that wasn't there.

"I know it's none of my business what you do in your free time," Mark said, "but starting Monday, your evening hours are scheduled with balloon rides. So tonight is the best time for ice cream. With all that advertising we did and then losing a pilot, our schedule was a little backed up. But now that you're here, Kyle, we're back on track."

"You want to come, too, Mr. Zimmer?" Michael asked, his face exuberant that ice cream was in his near future.

Mark chuckled. "No. I have plans with the fam. Grandkids are coming over. But you go ahead, have a big scoop of caramel nut swirl for me."

Nikki brushed a strand of hair from her face. "Okay, then. Michael and I will see you later this evening, Kyle."

She led Michael away and left Kyle standing there with Mark, who crossed his arms when Nikki disappeared. "This business needs you or else I might have sent you packing as soon as I learned of your omission. On the other hand, I understand the reason."

"You do?" How much did the man know, if anything at all?

"Sure. There are issues between the two of you that need to be resolved. I didn't place you at first—I'm new to this business—but now I realize you were the guy on that balloon with her brother when he was killed."

Kyle frowned. This wasn't exactly the way he wanted to make his start here, but what had he expected?

"Yep. That's me, the last person to see him alive." Kyle wasn't sure if he wanted to know the answer, but he couldn't keep from asking. "What else did she tell you?"

"She blames you for his death. Not in so many words, but I can tell."

What a surprise.

A breeze swept through the warehouse from the door Nikki had left open and ruffled the balloon envelope splayed across the floor.

Under the circumstances, maybe Kyle couldn't work here after all. "And what do *you* think?"

"Her brother made his own decision. We all know the risks."

Kyle sighed. Mark was the first person who didn't blame him, or so it seemed. "Thanks. I appreciate hearing you say that."

"I hope you appreciate my next words, too. She didn't ask for you to show up today. That girl's gone through enough. Make sure you understand the risks where she's concerned."

We all know the risks.

Kyle had a strange feeling that he hadn't counted all the risks involved in seeing Nikki again.

Chapter 3

Nikki stumbled through the front door of the modest home she'd shared with her mother since her father died, and she tossed her bag on the sofa.

"Michael... Mom..." she called. Likely they were already eating supper. Her mother hated for her to be late and it was already almost six-thirty. Kyle would be here in fifteen minutes.

Thank goodness she'd had all the errands to run—pick up a prescription, return the movie rentals, grab the stuff on Mom's grocery list and a thousand other things—or she would have been stuck at the warehouse working with him. This was her business, after all. But she'd needed this afternoon away to process his return.

Michael ran around the corner, his lips tinted reddish-orange with tomato sauce.

Spaghetti night.

Michael gave her a squeeze. "You'd better hurry and

eat or Grandma won't let you get ice cream with me and Uncle Kyle."

Ah, the appeal of living at home. Checking her sarcasm, Nikki reminded herself she stayed here for Michael's sake and for her mother's. Certainly not for her own.

Her mother appeared at the same moment Nikki released a weighty sigh. Why had she thought she'd return in time to break the news of Kyle's arrival to Mom before Michael did? Then again, her nephew was excited and eager to see Uncle Kyle again, and Nikki hadn't been thinking straight *because* she'd seen Kyle again.

"Sorry I'm late," Nikki said and brushed past her mother.

Her mother leaned against the doorway, her posture confirming her struggle with her particular brand of melancholy. Nikki would have preferred that she stand there with her hands on her hips.

Should she call Kyle and tell him not to come? No, wait. In her rush to exit the warehouse, she hadn't asked for his phone number, which would have been awkward at best, given she wanted to remain outside his reach. For now. Plus, he was probably already on his way.

She slid into her seat at the dinner table that was covered in a white linen tablecloth, and she scooped spaghetti onto her plate to be a good example for Michael. A good example for her mother, who clearly hadn't touched her food.

"Something bothering you, Mom?" Questioning the obvious was their way.

Michael hopped back into his seat and chomped on a meatball.

"I'm sure you know the answer to that." Her mother sat in the seat across from her, elbows on the table. "Why didn't you tell me?"

"That we're getting ice cream?"

"That Kyle Morgan is back and you're letting him work with you again."

Nikki wasn't the only one who blamed Kyle for Jordan's death. She chewed on the spaghetti.

Needs salt. But she didn't dare season it in front of her mother. The salt and pepper shakers were placed on the table for decoration only, not as a means to insult the cook. Nikki had given herself the afternoon to catch her breath, as it were, but she was in no way ready to be pressed for answers regarding any questions about Kyle.

Besides, no matter what Nikki said to her mother, she would disagree. "I'm sorry about that. Didn't think it was a big deal, though I had planned to mention it when I got home, and now that I'm here, you already know."

She twirled more spaghetti on her fork then quickly shoved it in her mouth to distract attention from her trembling hands. What would her mother think if she had known Nikki's strong reaction to seeing Kyle again? She still hadn't figured it out herself. She'd thought he was a memory she'd just as soon forget and nothing more. But she had that wrong.

All wrong.

Her mother frowned and glanced at Michael. "I'm not sure how I feel about this."

You don't have to see him every day. Why do you care? "Don't worry. I'll find out why he's back."

Nikki had the sense that Kyle had hoped for a more positive welcome from her. They had plenty to discuss, but not in front of Michael.

"Tell me what you find out." Her mother stood and scraped Michael's empty plate onto her still-full one. "But if you're going to get ready you should do it now."

Midchew, Nikki looked at her mother. "Get ready?"

"Fix your makeup. Comb your hair. Make yourself presentable."

For Kyle?

Nikki swallowed more than spaghetti when her mother disappeared into the kitchen. She swallowed the lump that had grown past ignoring since Kyle had suddenly appeared in her life as though ready to take off where he'd left things, sans her brother.

Michael stared at her across the table. Sauce covered his blue-and-green-striped polo. "Better change into another shirt, little buddy."

She gasped. Kyle had called him *little buddy* this afternoon. Somewhere in her subconscious she obviously decided she liked the endearment. "I mean, Sheriff. You'd better change your shirt, Sheriff Michael."

At that, Michael slid from his chair and disappeared down the hallway.

Someone knocked at the door. *He's here already? It's only 6:26.*

Her mother was right. Nikki needed—no, wanted—to prepare herself to see Kyle. What was wrong with her? Her appearance didn't matter. This wasn't a date. She tried to act as if she didn't care, but that was a lie. She reminded herself that he'd hurt her, hurt her family in ways a person just didn't forget, and still her heart jumped at the thought of him standing on the other side of that door.

She was a traitor.

"Mom, can you get that for me, please?" On second thought, no telling what her mother would say to the man. "Never mind, I'll get it."

Nikki paused in the foyer and glimpsed her reflection in the mirror. *Crumpled* didn't describe her look. A few spots of tomato sauce had splattered her shirt, too. She would let him in then excuse herself for a few minutes to freshen up.

Hand on the doorknob, she felt moisture slide into her palms. She'd once loved this man. Then she'd blamed him.

Swinging the door open just as Kyle raised his fist for another knock, Nikki looked into those eyes again, and her heart stumbled at his wide triple grin.

He gazed down at her face and his eyes lingered on her clothes. "Spaghetti night. I used to love that."

Sitting at the local playground after they'd enjoyed a little too much ice cream, Kyle watched Michael play with a few other children while Nikki went to the restroom.

Michael ran up to Kyle, laughing and catching his breath. "Thanks for talking Aunt Nikki into letting us get ice cream. I owe you."

"No, Sheriff, I'm the one who owes you." He held up his palm for a high five.

Michael shook his head and fisted his hand. "Knuckles."

"Knuckles it is." Kyle responded in kind and they bumped knuckles.

"I'll think of how you can repay me." Michael smiled before bouncing back to the monkey bars.

Kyle chuckled, wishing he hadn't missed the past three years with the boy. He'd already tortured himself with guilt long enough, and there wasn't anything he could do about that now, except this. Coming back to Albuquerque and to Sky High to see Nikki and make things right.

How he could make things right by showing his face again, he wasn't sure. And whether or not she'd give him the chance remained to be seen, but he definitely owed Michael for tonight. If it weren't for Jordan's son, Kyle doubted he would have been given this time with Nikki. Thinking about her startled look when she'd first seen him was painful, so he tried to erase that from his thoughts.

It wasn't easy.

Watching the playground, he spotted Nikki exit the ladies' room. She ran to Michael and lifted him, swirling him around. Her familiar laughter wrapped around Kyle, uncovering a host of vivid images. He shared her pain—returning brought the memories back to the surface and made them raw to the touch.

Holding Michael's hand, she led the protesting child toward Kyle. That must be his signal that their evening was ending, and soon. So far, Michael's presence had kept any serious discussion out of reach.

Nikki plopped onto the park bench next to Kyle and tugged a tissue from her purse. She wiped the smudges from Michael's face.

Admiration squeezed Kyle's insides. "You're good for him, you know that?"

Nikki stiffened and peered at Kyle. "Thank you for the evening, Kyle, but it's time to go home now."

"Aw, do we have to?" Michael hopped from the bench and scowled. "We just got here."

"Come on, little buddy." Kyle lifted Michael onto his shoulders. "You need to get Aunt Nikki home and into bed or she won't be able to get up in the morning for church."

"Did you forget I'm the sheriff?" Michael gave him a playful scowl then giggled as Kyle led the way back to his Denali, Nikki walking twice as fast to keep up.

The ride home uneventful, Nikki didn't invite him inside but asked him to wait for her on the porch. Was she getting Michael settled in? Maybe her mother didn't feel comfortable seeing Kyle.

Fortunately, Nikki had left him with a cold glass of lemonade on the warm August evening. The porch swing creaked under his weight as he rocked back and forth, dreading the moment when she would appear again. What would she say? Would she tell him to leave, after all?

What was worse, depending on her questions, he wasn't quite sure that he had any answers he could put into words. Light beamed from the crack in the door as it opened. She quietly shut it and crept over to sit next to him.

This close to her on the porch swing felt so peaceful, but it belied the conversation he knew was coming. Albuquerque, Sky High Balloons, Nikki and Michael magnified that he longed to have back all he'd lost, though he could never recover his best friend.

What sort of man didn't fulfill his promise? Kyle couldn't stand to think that he'd been that man. Maybe he'd fled the scene, a coping mechanism, as it were, but he could no longer avoid facing Jordan's sister.

Nikki's soft lavender perfume wrapped around him, reminding him of the only time he'd ever looked at her as more than a friend. Jordan's voice came back to him now. Afraid that Kyle would hurt his sister as he'd done some other girls, Jordan had drawn the line in the proverbial sand with her.

In the end, though, Jordan had elicited a promise from Kyle.

Next to him, Nikki released a long sigh. Kyle suspected she didn't know what to ask, where to start. He'd remedy that, but he knew bringing up Jordan's death would be painful for them both.

"Before he died, Jordan made me promise to watch over you and Michael. To help you with the business." Kyle would do that now, before he left to compete in the Gordon Bennett. Part of another promise to Jordan he was sure Nikki wouldn't appreciate. He'd have to tell her at some point. Just not tonight.

The porch swing stopped. "Does it look like I need your help?" she asked.

Kyle could barely make out her features in the dim light, and so he didn't know exactly how to respond.

"Okay, don't answer that," she added. "Why now, Kyle? Why, after you disappeared for three years, did you suddenly show up—"

Before she could draw another breath to voice her next twenty questions, Kyle interrupted. "I'm sorry. I messed up, okay? I won't make excuses for my actions, but will you give me the chance to keep that promise to Jordan?"

"You and Jordan should have considered the ramifications when you decided to enter that race. You should have considered how the rest of us would be affected if something happened, which it did."

Kyle had already heard this before, and he knew she was right, but it was too late for her brother. He also knew she needed to say the words, though how she held her emotions in check, he didn't know.

Nikki took a sip of her lemonade. "You can help with the business because Mark likes you, Michael adores you and we need you."

"You mean, Sheriff Michael," he said.

That elicited a small grin the way he'd hoped.

"But as to the other part of the promise," she said, the grin flattening out, "I don't need you to watch over me. I'm much stronger now after being on my own, and trusting you that much again isn't something I'm willing to do."

Chapter 4

Floating three thousand feet above the Rio Grande, Nikki smiled and congratulated the couple—Kathryn and Russ—who enjoyed a balloon ride on their twenty-fifth anniversary. Sky High specialized in weddings and anniversaries and romantic occasions of all kinds, so this was nothing new for Nikki. But this week had been almost unbearable. True to his word, Mark had managed to increase their bookings with his marketing savvy, but she suspected this was especially easier with the growing anticipation of the fiesta.

Regardless of the reason, Nikki had had her fill of romantic balloon rides this week. Anniversaries and one honeymooning couple. She'd done well to hold things together so far, but something about this couple chipped away at her.

"I've always wanted to do this," Kathryn said to Nikki, but her bright, passionate smile was for her husband. No doubt there.

"I'm happy for you," Nikki said.

Kathryn's eyes shimmered, and she brushed at the corners. "Sorry, we've just been through so much together, and I'm still in love with this man."

Nikki plastered her smile in place, knowing that any other day she'd feel warmth swelling in her chest, happy for this couple and their successful marriage. But a cloud shadowed her heart and mind. What was the matter with her?

Kathryn gained her composure and turned her attention on Nikki as though she felt guilty for enjoying a happy life, or perhaps that was simply Nikki's interpretation. She hoped her less-than-stellar mood wasn't that apparent.

"Are you married?" the woman asked.

Heat infused Nikki's cheeks, though this wasn't the first time she'd heard the question, and given the romance and ambience of the rides, the question always seemed to surface eventually. Kathryn hadn't meant anything by it, but today the inquiry felt intrusive.

Nikki adjusted her windbreaker. "No, I've just been too busy." *No time to meet anyone.* Anyone new, that was. Someone besides Kyle.

She had no idea why she thought she needed to give Kathryn an excuse, and she hoped the questions would stop there. Nikki sensed that Kathryn wanted to probe further. Enamored of her own blessed union, she wanted the world to experience what she had. Nikki didn't blame her for that, and in truth, she was a little jealous. If only every relationship could emanate the same love and joy these two shared.

Russ hadn't looked at Nikki since his wife had started babbling on about the thrill of his gift to her, and he took Kathryn's hand, bringing it to his lips.

Nikki fully expected to see that—any man who arranged for something special like this usually played the romance to the fullest. She'd seen it enough times.

Sunrise or sunset—the beginning of their lives together or the end—it made no difference.

But Nikki had never been affected the way she was at this moment. Why now? It forced her thoughts somewhere she'd rather not go. Though she'd grown to care for Kyle as more than a friend over the years, she'd been successful at keeping that to herself. He'd never returned her feelings that way. Never even looked at her that way back when Jordan was alive.

When he left, she'd released the feelings she'd harbored for Kyle, or so she'd thought. A new darker emotion had taken up residence in her heart. His sudden appearance a week ago stirred up all the old anger and resentment, and yet the fact that he came back, that he was here, kindled the warm light inside her as well—a light that shined in all the dark places, and that disturbed her.

All her confusing emotions left her winded.

Kyle left her gasping for air, and she couldn't decide if she hated him or…still loved him.

Russ cast a glance her way, startling her, and she realized she was staring. She knew when to turn her back, give them some privacy, but she just couldn't tear her eyes away when he tipped his wife's chin up just so and leaned in for a tender and gentle kiss—a kiss that showed how much he cherished this woman.

Nikki felt her own eyes well with tears and that was when she managed to give Russ and Kathryn the privacy they deserved. She forced herself around to lean against the basket, but instead of looking down at the city of Albuquerque drifting by below them, she closed her eyes.

After a few steadying breaths, she managed to open them again and focus on her surroundings—rising above it all in a hot-air balloon also took her breath away and had never failed to leave her in awe, even after spending her whole life in this business. In that way, and despite the tragedies in her life, she also knew that God had greatly blessed her, and a scripture floated over her heart.

Oh, Lord, our Lord, how majestic is Your name in all the earth...

She couldn't remember a more gorgeous evening for a balloon ride, and she allowed her thoughts to drift back to more happy times—those times when her father had taken her up as a child.

She was too young to see over the basket, so her father had held her up so she could see—something they discouraged in the balloon-ride business for safety reasons. At first the height had scared her. She remembered those emotions—the overwhelming fear—as if she were back in time. As if her father's protective arms were around her now, comforting her and making her feel safe and secure.

But he wasn't here. He'd died of a heart attack eight years ago. While she treasured those memories, they magnified the hole left in her life after losing both her father and then her brother.

She was stronger now, sure. Being on her own, though she still had her mother, had been good for her in that way, but the loneliness still followed her. Strange how losing two of the men she loved had left a gaping abyss in her heart, and the return of another man whom she secretly loved before only magnified that chasm.

Nikki opened the propane valve to flame the air inside the envelope—as she'd done intermittently throughout the ride—keeping the balloon at this altitude and moving with this wind direction and speed.

The sun began its descent into the horizon, producing colorful orange-and-pink hues. Nikki made the mistake of turning around to face the couple. They were caught up in a loving embrace. Nikki swallowed and turned her back on them once again before they noticed her unbidden attention.

Seeing them brought Kyle to the forefront of her thoughts once more—working with him was going to be tougher than she imagined. She could clap herself on the back— her efforts to avoid the man this past week had been successful. She and Kyle had been like the old adage about two ships passing in the night, only they were two hot-air balloons passing at dawn and dusk.

Sometimes literally.

She grappled with the fact that he was here serving her up a stark reminder of everything she'd lost almost on a daily basis. As much as she wanted to avoid him, she was keenly aware of his presence in her life, though from a distance. He was somehow with her all the time anyway—in her thoughts.

In my heart...

She wasn't ready to deal with him right now. There was too much going on in her life. Add to that, Mark had dropped subtle hints that Sky High needed to enter the fiesta competitions. So far, she'd avoided that discussion with him.

She'd never actually competed in the competitions, but rather Sky High offered more rides during the fiesta— the largest ballooning event in the world. And since the rides were in such demand with hundreds of thousands of visitors descending upon Albuquerque for the fiesta, they charged more, as well. But Jordan and Kyle had been the ones to race, competing in the gas-balloon race—the American Challenge—to see who could travel the longest distance. The last time they'd competed, they'd won.

The next year, they'd entered the Gordon Bennett.

At the thought of the race that had ended her brother's life, she squeezed her eyes shut. As to Mark's hints about racing, she told herself that her mother couldn't handle it. But Nikki didn't have the heart for it either, even though she might one day like to compete in honor of Jordan.

Truth was, business hadn't been so good until the past few weeks, and she needed to build it back up if she was ever going to sell it, getting as much money as it was worth, so she could free them from the memories and start over somewhere else. It would help if someone would call her on the résumé she'd sent out to hundreds, if not thousands of businesses and placed on internet job boards.

Other than running this business and piloting balloons, her father had encouraged her to get a degree, and she'd complied, finishing out four years in accounting and getting her CPA. She'd gone back to working on people's taxes part-time in addition to the balloon business, but her focus remained on the joy of piloting balloons—a joy she'd lost three years ago.

Though leaving it all behind and starting over somewhere seemed like the best plan, a battle raged in her head and heart.

She shoved it aside to focus on landing the balloon in the approaching field. The landowner had been giving permission for Sky High Balloons to land in his fields for years. After she pulled the cord that allowed hot air to escape the envelope, the balloon began its slow descent. She'd landed in this field so many times over the years she could almost do it in her sleep. The warehouse was positioned at just the right place for her balloons to take off and float on the right currents to carry them here.

Once on the ground, she felt the familiar vibration of her cell in her pocket and sneaked a quick peek. The text from her mother stated that Michael had gotten into a fistfight

at school. Why hadn't the principal called Nikki? Maybe
he had and couldn't reach her? Nikki fought the tears and
smiled at the couple, not wanting to spoil their evening together with her troubles. That certainly wouldn't garner
glowing recommendations for more business.

But she wasn't sure she could handle one more thing
going wrong today.

There!

Kyle spotted the van with the balloon trailer parked on
the shoulder of the highway, everyone milling about in the
waning daylight, waiting on the wrecker. But that could
be another forty-five minutes. He pulled onto the shoulder
behind the trailer and got out. When Mark had received
the call that the van had broken down, Kyle had insisted
on being the one to meet them and shuttle the clients back
to the warehouse and their own vehicles.

Though he was doing as he'd promised Jordan by helping with the business, he was failing miserably as far as
watching over Nikki was concerned. She'd made it clear
enough she didn't need him to take care of her, as Jordan
had requested, and she was right. This first week Kyle had
had second thoughts a thousand times. Maybe if he'd done
as promised three years ago, sure, but now, he was beginning to see that some promises held an expiration date.

Nikki had gone out of her way to avoid him, but what
did he expect? For her to welcome him with open arms?
No.

He deserved her reaction.

Growing up with her, he knew her almost as well as he'd
known her brother. Given a little time, she might open her
life up to him again. Given time, she might forgive him,
stop blaming him for her brother's death, something he'd
only suspected until it was confirmed by Mark.

And then what? Kyle would tell her that he was racing in the Gordon Bennett again? Sure. That would go over well. He was beginning to think he was a real cad for turning up again, only to announce his plans, but he had to do this. In his heart, he knew it would mean closure for both of them. He had to keep this one last promise to Jordan— to race and finish in the Gordon Bennett.

Winning would be even better.

As Kyle made his way to the broken-down vehicle, David left the group and met Kyle halfway, thrusting out his hand. "I'm glad to see you. I have a date tonight, and I'm already late."

"And the ride couple is celebrating their anniversary. I hope this didn't ruin it for them." He clapped David on the back in passing and made his way toward Nikki.

She remained engaged in conversation with the couple, whom she then introduced to Kyle as Kathryn and Russ. The easy way she shared their names, and the sincere smile she gifted them with, reminded him all over again of her compassion. How much she always cared about people, even complete strangers. The way the pair smiled and laughed, held hands, told him that a broken-down vehicle hadn't dampened their evening at all, especially while in Nikki Alexander's company.

She'd obviously endeared herself to this couple. Just as she'd endeared herself to him all over again without even trying.

"So you're here to cart them back to their vehicle?" she asked. Though she kept her smile in place, Kyle didn't miss the wariness in her eyes. Her need to keep her distance from him.

"Something like that," he said. He and David worked to hitch the balloon trailer onto the working vehicle. Kyle handed off the keys for the other working fifteen-passenger van to David.

"David will take all of you back." He glanced at his watch. "I don't think it's a good idea to leave the van just sitting here. I'll wait for the wrecker. Shouldn't be too much longer."

"Oh, no. That's too much to ask," she said. "You go on with David and Lenny. This was my ride and I'll see it through to the end."

David was already ushering the couple to the van when he glanced back, impatience registering on his face.

Kyle chuckled. "I think David's in a hurry. He's already late for a hot date. I don't feel comfortable with you waiting here by yourself, especially since it's getting dark. I'm here to help if I can, and besides, I'm sure Michael is anxious to see you. I'll call David to come pick me up if the wrecker service won't drop me off."

Kyle admitted he'd been anxious to see her, too. He didn't realize it would be so difficult to spend time with her, or that he'd *need* to spend time with her.

Her features fell and she pressed a shaky hand over her eyes. Seeing her like this, his stomach felt as if he'd suddenly dropped from the sky. Kyle stepped forward and reached out, almost touching her shoulder, but he quickly withdrew his hand.

"Everything okay?" Somehow he managed to keep his voice steady.

She dropped her hand, revealing residual moisture in her soft eyes. Gorgeous eyes. Something inside him stirred. Before this moment, he'd never allowed himself to linger on them for too long.

In that way.

Couldn't think of her like that. Could he maintain that distance when Jordan was no longer around, reminding him? Did it even matter, considering her obvious reluctance to let him in?

A strand of her dark hair whipped across her face. "Michael got in trouble at school."

"Who's going with me?" David rushed up to them.

Nikki stared at Kyle, long and hard. In her eyes he read her struggle over whether or not to allow herself to need him. At least this one time, she *did* need him.

"It's okay. I've got this," he said. "You go. See to Michael."

Her frown lifted a little at the corner. "Thank you."

And then she turned her back to him and followed David. They climbed into the vehicle, and David steered it onto the highway. Kyle watched it disappear, darkness quickly approaching. He'd been a little bit of an opportunist, wanting to use this chance to help Nikki.

To see her.

He wished that her smile would run deep for him, as it had with the couple, if she ever smiled at him at all. How he missed what they'd had together, the three of them, before Jordan's death.

Tired of waiting on the wrecker, Kyle opened the cab of the van to release the hood. He'd have a look, see if it was a simple fix, but even as he stared at the engine, he saw Nikki's face instead.

What am I doing back here, trying to fix something that can't be fixed? Trying to keep a promise broken long ago?

Chapter 5

Weary to the bone, it was almost nine o'clock by the time Nikki steered into the driveway.

Anxious to see Michael, she shoved through the garage door into the kitchen. *Oh, Jordan—your son needs you.*

The lights were out in the kitchen except for the one over the sink. Nikki's heart fell. She'd held on to hope that her mother would keep Michael up long enough for Nikki to talk to him. When Jordan had named Nikki as guardian instead of their mother should anything happen to him, Nikki had balked at first. But eventually she'd agreed to it because her mother wouldn't be in any condition to raise a young child if the worst happened. Her mother and father had waited later in life to start a family, and her mother was approaching her mid-sixties as it was.

Nikki had never regretted that decision, but for the most part, they raised Michael together.

Releasing a long breath, she set her purse on the counter. On the drive home, she'd worked on what to say to her nephew, whom she loved like a son, but she hadn't come up with much. Raising a child had to be the hardest job in the world.

So, she'd prayed. Mostly, she wanted to gather him in her arms when she got home. She'd already phoned the school principal and scheduled an appointment tomorrow morning just before lunch. Michael was so young, and it stunned her to hear the news about his brawl with another boy. But maybe when she saw him and talked to him about it, the whole incident would turn out to be just a minor spat between two second graders. Everything blown out of proportion. That had to be it.

Still, she couldn't help but feel as if she was failing miserably in raising him. She crept through the house and took a step toward Michael's room.

"He's asleep." Her mother's voice startled her.

Nikki turned to see her sitting in a chair in the living room, the shadows skewing her features. "I thought you'd be asleep, too. I just wanted to check on him. Maybe he's awake."

"It was a hard day for him. He thinks he's in trouble."

"He *is* in trouble," Nikki said.

The principal hadn't gone into specifics, but Nikki had been hard-pressed to believe that Michael would start a fight. More likely he'd defended himself. And Nikki would defend him if it came to that.

"He needs a father figure, and he'd have one if it weren't for Kyle."

Her mother's harsh words surprised her.

"Why'd he come back?" her mother asked before Nikki could form a response to her earlier words.

"I…don't know, Mom." Kyle had shared his reasons with her, but she hadn't found a way to tell her mother. Nor was she sure Kyle was telling her everything. "But we both know that Jordan knew the risks. He made his own decision."

Nikki left her mother and headed to Michael's room, hating the pressure squeezing her chest. She had blamed Kyle for Jordan's death, too, all these years. Just like her mother—but hearing the words spoken aloud, the harsh reality behind them—how could she hold that over Kyle? And yet, she did. She couldn't help herself.

He could have done something to save Jordan that day. She had always believed that. Nikki shoved those morbid thoughts away to focus on Michael. Quietly, she opened the door to his room to peek in on him. The hall light chased away enough darkness for her to see his sleeping form and his tear-stained cheeks.

Nikki wanted to rush to him, hug him, let him know she loved him. Tell him everything would be all right. But her mother was right—she should let him sleep. When she went back into the living room, her mother had already disappeared into her own room. Nikki grabbed her purse from the counter and remembered that Mark had given her a small building-blocks toy for Michael, but with the vehicle breaking down, she'd forgotten to pick it up where he'd promised to leave it on his office desk.

Exhaustion poured over her. She didn't want to drive all the way back for it, but the toy might be just what she needed to give Michael to smooth things over after their talk. A reprimand, if needed, then the toy—not so much a reward as a gentle reminder that Michael was loved no matter what.

Nikki sighed and dug out her keys then let her mother know her plans to swing by the warehouse to pick up Mark's surprise for Michael.

On the drive over, she thought about her mother's words.

He needs a father figure, and he'd have one if it weren't for Kyle.

She could still see the anguish in her mother's face when she'd asked the question that Nikki also wanted to ask: *Why'd he come back?*

Why, indeed. Could it be as simple as what he'd told her—to finally keep his promise to Jordan? To watch over her and Michael?

Nikki didn't know why she struggled to accept his explanation—but maybe it had something to do with how he disappeared and had suddenly turned up again. In the end, she would sell the business and get a job somewhere else, doing something else. That would be best for her mother, Michael and for herself.

Pulling into the Sky High parking lot, she spotted Kyle's navy Denali still parked there, next to the van. This late? She figured he'd already have made it back by now and gone home.

She parked her minivan and made her way to the warehouse. She hadn't missed the concern in his eyes when Kyle insisted that he stay behind for the wrecker while she went home to Michael, and she tried to ignore his thoughtfulness.

Let him in now, and she might crumble.

She'd spent so much energy blaming him, just like her mother, and now that he was back for who knew how long, she had to face everything again. Face things she'd avoided since Jordan's death.

Nikki entered the building quietly. A radio blasted contemporary Christian music, drowning out her footfalls.

Kyle was crouched over a bright yellow balloon envelope, fingering a rip. Their newest balloon!

The one Jordan had purchased just before his death. He'd named it *Intrepid*. Daring and fearless, just like him.

She covered her mouth, stifling her gasp. He angled his head toward her, his gaze pinning her in place, his expression one she'd seen many times growing up—that was, when he'd been caught. His culpable look sent a rush of memories sweeping over her.

Unfortunately, they brought all her old buried feelings for him to the front, too.

Although one of her balloons lay on the floor rendered useless, happiness rushed through her. That, and suspicion.

"What are you doing?" she asked.

Kyle stood, momentarily stunned at Nikki's appearance. The look in her eyes—as if they'd shared a moment from the past lost to both of them—had stirred something inside. But it had quickly morphed into an emotion he didn't understand, considering her accusing tone.

"What? You can't really think I had anything to do with this."

Her brows knitted and she shook her head a little. "No, of course not."

She blinked up at him and then down at the envelope. He knew she'd been suspicious of him. Even if it had only been a fleeting thought, the idea cut him.

Putting aside the hurt, and the ripped balloon, he turned his attention to her. "How's Michael?"

She came all the way into the room and dropped to her knees, lifting the material where it was torn, a slight tremble in her hand. "I don't know. He was asleep when I got home. I came back here to get a toy that Mark wanted to give him. What happened, Kyle?"

"Instead of going home, I came inside and walked in on this. Mark mentioned someone had caused a few problems before. He said it was just some kids' pranks." Kyle wasn't so sure about that. This was serious. "But how did they get into the trailer to pull this out? Obviously they did this not long after David parked the trailer with your balloon inside."

Frowning, Nikki appeared to puzzle over his question.

"Where did you find Mark, anyway?" Kyle inwardly cringed—the question hadn't come out right. It sounded too accusing. "I mean, he doesn't seem like someone who's been around the balloon business for long." At least in Albuquerque. All he had to go on there was the fact that Mark hadn't recognized Kyle's name, but he wasn't about to say that. He would come off sounding completely arrogant.

Nikki rose to face him, her eyes glistening beneath the flickering warehouse lights. "Mark retired and sold his RV business. He and Dad were friends years ago. I ended up firing Nathan and wanted someone I could trust, and Mark knows something about making a business successful. He built his up and then sold it for a nice profit. He's been here a couple of years now."

"Wait, who is Nathan?"

"I hired Nathan after…" Her words trailed off.

After Jordan died and Kyle left. He was an idiot to ask the question.

"And you didn't think you could trust him?"

"I didn't mean it like that. Nathan was a recent college graduate, and he just wasn't up to the task. How could anyone replace Jordan? Nathan messed up a few times. I decided I didn't need anyone to help, so I tried to do it all myself—schedule the flights and pilot them, too. I went from three pilots to just me, and I had no time to grieve." Nikki covered her face for a moment.

Kyle took a step forward, wanting to comfort her, but he sensed she wouldn't want that. He was such a jerk to leave her in that position.

Nikki recovered and dropped her hand. "I almost lost

the business completely. Then I found Mark to help me build it back up. And we had Gil as another pilot but he moved. And then you showed up."

"Mark seems like a good guy." Kyle was glad she'd continued her explanation, though she'd faltered a little there. Somehow, they both needed to move forward. "So, about Nathan, you don't think he's holding some sort of grudge, do you?"

"Not likely. If he is, he sure waited long enough." Nikki's brows twitched together.

Kyle didn't want to worry her. He'd talk to Mark more about this later. Had she even told Mark about Nathan? "I'll make sure the balloon is repaired. Don't worry. Mark and I will get new locks on everything. A security system, too."

Maybe install a security camera.

Nikki's face visibly relaxed. Kyle had always thought she was beautiful with her shiny, thick dark hair. Her vibrant, rich blue eyes. But with all the years of practice barring his thoughts from going there where she was concerned, it was tough, letting go of his control. The thing was, he had no doubt that he was drawn to her as much more than a friend, otherwise there would be nothing for him to fight. No concern about losing control over his emotions or thoughts.

Now that he admitted it, the question remained. Should he or shouldn't he pursue her? Considering the tragedy that would always stand between them, he shouldn't. But he couldn't resist the look in her eyes that still flickered behind all her distrust and resentment.

Behind the hurt.

He took a step closer, wanting to tell her again how sorry he was for everything.

She drew in a breath. "Thank you," she said.

Kyle sensed the difficulty she had in expressing her appreciation. "Can I ask you something?"

A small grin broke through her frown, though her eyes were still troubled. "Yeah?"

"For a minute there, you thought I was responsible for ripping the balloon. Like I did it on purpose. I mean, it crossed your mind."

She shook her head. "I already told you no."

"Come on, Nikki. How long have we known each other?"

Her cheeks colored and she averted her gaze for a few seconds before looking back.

"Why?" he asked. "Why would you think even for a second that I mean to harm you?" Maybe he should have kept that question to himself. That could open up a festering wound again, one he wished would heal.

She shoved her dark hair behind her head and twisted it in a knot. "I just… I don't know. My suspicions weren't directed at you, specifically. It's almost like someone wants to sabotage my efforts to sell the business, but that can't be true. I only just decided to sell right before you came."

Sell the business? "What did you say?" The question slipped out before he could comprehend her statement.

"A few weeks before you showed up, I decided to sell the business. It's a decision that's been a long time coming."

Too stunned for words, he just stared at her. If she sold then she might be out of his life forever when he was just beginning to realize he wanted her in it. He'd been such a fool, leaving the way he had. Staying away for so long.

Nikki lifted her gaze to the ceiling and allowed it to roam over the warehouse. "I remember when Daddy first decided to grow his balloon business from something he did in the mornings and evenings to his full-time job. He had such big plans."

"And he made them happen." Kyle crossed his arms and watched her, enjoying seeing this side of her again.

"Yes. He worked training pilots, too." She glanced over at him, warmth in her eyes. "Finally, he had enough business that this took all his time. He loved every minute of it."

She ran her fingers across a shelf holding a few old propane burners and other junk from the good old days when her father was still alive. He saw in her eyes then what he'd believed and the reasons her words stunned him. This place was in her blood.

She loved it here.

"You can't sell. You'll regret that for the rest of your life." He had some nerve, considering that he'd so easily walked away from it, and feared he might hear the same from Nikki.

She stiffened at his words.

Here it comes. He deserved her retort.

When she didn't reply and instead hung her head, Kyle felt like the heel he was. "Nikki," he whispered and took a step closer. "You love this place too much. Michael loves it here, too. It's in your blood. I can't believe you're going to sell."

Then she angled her head his way. "Believe it."

She rushed by him, heading for the exit. He grabbed her arm, gently swinging her around. "I'll buy it from you, then. Pay you top dollar, if that's what you really want."

Yeah, right. He couldn't even afford his own balloon.

Confusion and incredulity creased her forehead as she huffed. "If I have a choice, I won't sell it to you, Kyle." She shook her head, glancing at the door as though she couldn't wait to escape.

"Why not?"

"Look, you don't owe me anything. I release you from the promise you made to my brother three years ago, okay? You don't have to buy the business to ease your conscience."

He felt that falling sensation in his gut again. "I'm not here to ease my conscience."

"Aren't you?" Her severe frown loosened and her face relaxed. "I don't blame you anymore. It was wrong for me to hold you responsible for Jordan's death. I realize that now."

Kyle released a pent-up breath. "You don't know how much I've wanted to hear you say that."

Nikki sent him a weak grin, but by the hope it ignited inside Kyle, it might as well have been a thousand-watt smile.

She tilted her head. "Walk me to my car?"

The girl could do him in if he let her. He might have fallen for her hard before, if Jordan hadn't stood in his way. Would Jordan disapprove now?

Kyle nodded and followed her out to the parking lot. After she hit the locks, he opened the door to her car for her. She paused and looked up at the starry night. Kyle joined her, his attention drifting to Polaris—the North Star—and Little Bear then back down at Nikki. Angling her head the way she did, he got a good view of her long and graceful neck.

He didn't want this moment to end, and he knew that voicing his thoughts would end it, but they needed to be said. He wanted to get this out of the way in case he could recover even a small portion of his friendship with her.

"Nikki." He sighed. "You should know I blamed myself, too." He always wondered if he could have done more to change the outcome, and he carried that deep regret with him every day. How could he expect Nikki to forgive him, when he couldn't even forgive himself?

Her somber expression returning, she focused on something beyond him. "I have to move on, for Michael's sake, and for Mom's. That's why I'm selling the business."

"What will you do then? You're not leaving the area, are you?"

"I've applied for a few jobs out of state, yes."

Oh. That far, huh.

He had no right to offer an opinion. "I'm sorry to hear that."

"Why, Kyle? You had your chance to put distance between yourself and all that happened. To gain perspective. You left and stayed away until a week ago."

"And I regretted every minute that I was away." Kyle couldn't help himself. He reached up, lifted a strand of her gorgeous, silky hair that had fallen loose. "It was a mistake."

An emotion he couldn't read stirred behind her eyes, then she shifted away from him and slid into the seat of her minivan. "Good night, Kyle."

She shut the door.

"Good night, Nikki."

Chapter 6

Kyle watched her drive away for the second time that day, knowing that she might soon be driving out of his life for good.

He could berate himself until the end of time on that one—he'd been the one to leave first. Trudging back into the warehouse, he carried a weight heavier than he'd carried before his decision to return to Albuquerque.

Nikki was selling. She was leaving.

He needed to accept that. Let her go. What an idiot he was to come back and expect something from her. Was she right in accusing him of his need to ease his own conscience? A little bit, sure, but wasn't a man's conscience that part of his heart that directed him toward doing what was right?

What was wrong with that?

Maybe if his coming back was right for him but wrong for Nikki and Michael, then he was acting self-centered.

Maybe he should talk to her about that the next time he saw her—ask her point-blank if she wanted him to go.

The balloon envelope spread out on the warehouse floor rippled in the breeze from the fan above and helped him to release the punishing thoughts. He needed to inspect the balloon for other damage. There could be more cuts, but at the very least, this entire panel would need to be replaced. He'd ask Mark about the inspection schedule, but regardless, he'd inspect their two other balloons immediately.

As for *Intrepid*—Jordan's balloon—he'd have to call a repair technician in on this.

With the business trying to pick up, they sure didn't need to lose a balloon. He hadn't asked about the financial situation, but buying another one was a huge expense. Did their insurance cover vandalism? He hadn't pressed Nikki on the vandalism problem because he hadn't wanted to worry her too much.

He hoped that after tonight, after getting things out in the open, he and Nikki could move on with their lives. Somewhere in the mix of it all, a small part of him wanted to move on with her in a more personal way. In the few moments they'd spent together, the thoughts pushed forward little by little, breaking through the prison where he'd kept them because of her brother. He'd returned with a small measure of hope that she would call him friend again. Wanting something more, asking for something more was too much.

He knew that, and yet...

He shook the thought from his mind, and back to a problem he knew he could handle. In the morning he'd make sure to get more details from Mark about the previous vandalism. The guy had all but brushed aside what he claimed was simply a kid's prank.

But things had just turned serious. If Kyle didn't find

out what was going on here, someone could end up getting hurt, a kid's prank or not. Intentional or not. They needed to call the police, if Mark hadn't already.

Maybe it would be best if Nikki sold out and left after all.

Though it was late, Kyle got on his cell and called Rich Keller, an old friend whom Kyle had counted on for years to repair balloon envelopes. Chances were, Sky High still used Rich for repairs. Kyle hadn't spoken to Rich in three years, but Rich didn't have a reason to hold a grudge the way Nikki did.

The phone rang until it went to voice mail, and Kyle left a detailed message. Kyle stayed up late into the night hours combing the balloon for other damage. By midnight he was exhausted and had to admit he could do a better job in the light of day. He did his best to store the balloon out of the way for the morning rides, grateful they still had two more balloons, both of which were locked up as they were supposed to be, just like this one should have been.

How did the vandals get to this one?

Confused about what was going on, Kyle also called Mark to leave a voice mail, but he couldn't leave a message. The voice mailbox was full. Kyle chuckled. Either the guy didn't clear out his mailbox or he was extremely popular.

Kyle used the key Mark had given him and unlocked the office. He left a big note that he couldn't miss. Best thing he could do was show up here first thing in the morning, early enough to speak with Mark alone before clients arrived and the day got going.

On Mark's desk, Kyle noticed a box of interlocking bricks that, when put together, created a spaceship. Once put together, the toy would be a lot smaller than the box made it look. Funny that these things were still so popular. He'd loved to play with them when he was a kid, too.

Nikki had come back tonight for the toy but found Kyle instead. He'd distracted her. Even if she remembered the toy halfway home, he knew she wouldn't return, because she wouldn't want to see him.

If he really believed that, why was he still here? Kyle sighed and scraped his fingers through his hair, confusion racking his brain. Nothing was turning out the way he thought it would, the way he had hoped. How did he keep his promise to Jordan? How did he make amends to Nikki? How did he gain her trust again?

There seemed to be an abyss between them too big to cross—and Kyle almost wanted to give up. Almost.

He reminded himself that he was a pilot and there wasn't an abyss too big for him to cross when he used those skills to their fullest. Snatching up the box of toy blocks, he intended to deliver them in person like a fairy in the night for Nikki and Sheriff Michael to find in the morning.

And with them, he'd include a note to Nikki. One in which he'd tell her that if she wanted him out of her life for good, he would go.

Nikki slipped between the sheets, more exhausted than she'd been in ages.

That Kyle.

Her head against the pillow, she shut her eyes, seeing his face again, the intensity in his stark blue gaze as he'd touched her hair. Experiencing the unbidden joy that coursed through her.

For years, she would have given anything if he had done that. Given anything for him to see something more in her besides a friend. Seeing her as someone more than simply Jordan's sister.

And now, after everything that had happened, he'd

shown up with his grin, his gentle and kind ways with Michael, and even with her and… Nikki huffed and rolled to her side.

The anger and blame she'd held on to had protected her from the hurt his leaving had caused. And while he was away, it was enough to hold a grudge against him for his behavior. For his part in Jordan's death, though she wasn't exactly sure what that was. But when a person wanted forgiveness, and they showed that in everything they did and said, who was she to deny that person?

Even if that person was Kyle Morgan.

Nikki slowly exhaled. The Lord required her to forgive, regardless. Jesus had forgiven her, and she had to do the same for others.

But if you do not forgive men their sins, your Father will not forgive your sins. The familiar verse from Romans drifted through her heart. She knew well enough what to do—it was the how that she struggled with.

Lord, how do I forgive? How do I let go of the past?

She thought she knew how until Kyle showed up—she was making plans to leave. He'd come back wanting to fix things that were beyond repair, and she was trying to run away from it all.

But she had more to think about than herself. Her mother refused to see a doctor or a therapist or Christian counselor, but Nikki knew she was suffering with depression that had been spiraling deeper since Jordan's death. Nikki believed a change in scenery could be the answer, a clean break from everything that reminded them of their loss. That meant a break from Kyle, as well, and even if Nikki could get beyond the tumultuous emotions roiling inside where he was concerned, the fact remained she'd never get a chance with him.

That time had passed.

Jordan kept them apart before. He kept them apart now.

Grateful she didn't have a morning balloon ride to pilot, Nikki slipped into a fitful sleep.

She was awakened in the early morning anyway when her mother stepped into the room and set something on the bed next to her. Nikki peeked over her shoulder through slits in her sleepy eyes.

"What is it?" Nikki mumbled the question.

"You have a secret admirer." Her mother's tone left no question as to her displeasure. "He left something on the front porch."

Heart jolting her awake, Nikki rolled over to find a brown paper bag, her name written across the top in Kyle's artsy handwriting. Nikki was fully awake now and sat up, positioning her pillows just right.

Michael peered into the room. "Sheriff Michael here. I need to inspect that package."

Nikki paused. "You need to get ready for school."

He frowned. She had her appointment with his principal today, too, which almost brought a frown to her own face. "Come here, Sheriff," she said and scooted over so he could snuggle with her. "We'll look inside together."

He beamed a smile, and she noticed his slightly swollen lip, but she didn't mention it. When he climbed into bed, she hugged him. "I love you," she whispered.

"I love you, too—now, what's in the bag."

Nikki chuckled and unfolded the top, unsure what she might see inside. Suddenly, she worried it might be better to do this alone, but it didn't matter anymore when Michael's impatience won out, and he opened the top and peered inside.

He released an enormous gasp.

Nikki took her turn. The toy. She'd forgotten about it

last night—the entire reason she'd gone back to the warehouse.

She tugged the box from the sack and handed it over to Michael, who crawled from the bed. Before she could protest, he emptied the box on the floor, tiny bricks falling all over the place. Nikki glanced at the clock, grateful it was still early enough she didn't have to worry about getting him ready for school just yet.

When had Kyle delivered this? Early this morning before a balloon ride, or late last night? She started folding the sack but then felt something else inside and pulled out an envelope addressed to her, again in his familiar handwriting. She ran her finger over her name.

He'd written her a note? Why would he do that? She almost dreaded to read it.

She carefully tore the envelope and opened his letter. The fact that he'd taken time to write her like this touched her heart. Michael playing on the floor, she pressed her hand against her chest.

Mom leaned on the doorjamb, a smile barely tugging at the corner of her mouth as she watched Michael with the blocks. "I'll start breakfast," she said and disappeared.

Nikki became engrossed in Kyle's letter, in which he poured out his heart. Guys didn't usually do this, did they?

Kyle explained pretty much everything he'd already said about why he'd come back and again apologized for being a coward to begin with. Said that he'd struggled with Jordan's death, perhaps more than anyone, and then his new life stole time from him until he knew he had to come back.

I know I'm too late, really, to keep my promise to Jordan, but I'd like a chance to try, at least before you leave, if you'll give me that. Mostly, I wanted to give you a chance to tell me to go away, if that's what you believe is the best thing for you and Sheriff Michael.

A small laugh escaped at his last phrase. Tears sliding down her cheeks, she pressed the letter against her heart.

"Are you okay?" Michael placed his small hand on her arm.

She opened her eyes and smiled. "Sure. One thing you'll learn about girls as you get older—"

"They cry a lot. I know." Michael quickly forgot the conversation and planted himself back on the carpet to finish assembling the little building blocks.

Nikki laughed again and wiped at the tears. That Kyle. He not only knew how to fly balloons, filling them with air and lifting them sky-high, he knew how to lift a girl's spirits. On the downside, Nikki thought she'd known what was best for her and Michael, and for Mom, but now she wasn't sure at all. It wasn't as though she could send Kyle away, if she ever could.

Her mother appeared in the room again, eyeing the letter Nikki held. "Coffee's on."

No doubt, Mom would have no problem telling Kyle to disappear again.

Chapter 7

Kyle's crew on Saturday morning included a married couple in their mid-fifties, Randy and Kay Ellis, who were looking to get involved in ballooning. Serving on a balloon crew was one of the best places to get started. David was here, too, making sure all went smoothly. He was great at teaching others. Together, they positioned Kyle's balloon in the wide-open field next to the warehouse, where the Sky High balloons took off for their flights.

In the cool of the morning, Kyle wore a light jacket over his T-shirt. A gorgeous dawn had broken, the sky painted with colors Kyle didn't think he'd seen before, and the wind was less than 5 mph.

A perfect day for flying.

He could think of only one more thing—make that *person*—that could make the day any better. But he wouldn't see Nikki today—her clients had canceled on her.

One of Kyle's clients flashed him a flirtatious smile.

By the look of it, she and her friend might be a handful. He wished Mark had scheduled them to ride with Nikki instead of Kyle this morning.

The two attractive women waited alongside the activity, taking pictures of each other posing in front of the balloon as it filled with air, looking as if it grew right out of the earth. Once the envelope was upright and ready for takeoff, they asked Kyle to pose with one or the other of them in turn, as well, to which he'd obliged.

All part of the job.

The Ellises flashed him knowing grins, having fun at his expense.

When Nikki pulled into the parking lot across the way, Kyle was surprised to see her. Her crew had already gone. After uttering his apologies with a promise for a quick return, he jogged across the field to meet her.

Cell phone at her ear, she stepped from her vehicle and frowned.

As Kyle approached, he reminded himself he hadn't yet heard her response to the letter he'd given her earlier in the week and it was Saturday already. When he hadn't been piloting balloons, he'd been busy finishing up a contract programming project during the day and late at night. That, and working with Mark to oversee the installation of a security system and camera.

He'd hoped that no reply meant good news, though that was really holding on to false hope. No reply could mean anything at all.

He caught his breath. "I take it you heard."

"That my client canceled? Yeah," she said and blew a stray hair from her forehead. "What is wrong with my stupid phone? I didn't hear it ring and just now got the message."

Kyle leaned forward, peering into the backseat at Jordan's son. "Hey, Sheriff Michael."

Then it hit him.

He eyed Nikki. "You brought him along for a ride?"

"Wait here," she said to Michael and shut the door. "Mom wasn't feeling well. I left her in bed. I didn't think it would be a good idea to leave Michael. It's Saturday, so he doesn't have school. But he could wait here with Mark, except Mark isn't here yet. He told me he was coming in this morning to meet with the new pilot he hired. His name is Chase. Have you met him yet?"

"Not yet. I'm sorry to hear that she's sick."

"Thanks." Nikki's eyes were troubled. "I had no choice but to bring him. This time of morning isn't a good time to start calling babysitters. But since my clients canceled, I can take Michael home now. I don't want him to start dreaming about balloons."

Like your father? His father? Everyone in his family? Kyle kept the words to himself, hating that Nikki felt that way, but he understood. What had happened to her family wasn't the usual way of things by any stretch.

"I came over to ask if you'd like to ride with me today." He glanced back at *Daydreamer,* waiting and ready for flight, and the two women who waved at him from across the field. He could hear them calling his name from over here—that and their giggles.

Something about the scene sent an unpleasant tension through Kyle.

"Can we, please?" Michael had sneaked out of the vehicle on the other side.

Nikki gasped.

Michael's eyes were as bright as Kyle had ever seen them. Kyle couldn't imagine Nikki not giving in to those pleading eyes. Yep, it was in the family blood.

He would add to her dilemma if he could. "Yes, please, Nikki?"

Nikki frowned as she looked over his shoulder at the waiting balloon and passengers. "Could you have another reason for wanting me along? Say, to act as your protector or something?"

"Who says I need protection?" He grinned.

Her eyes danced with mischief. "Okay, I'm sure you're right. You can handle those two gorgeous babes by yourself. So, I'll just take Michael home."

"No!" Michael cried. "I want to go up with Uncle Kyle. It's been forever since I've been in a balloon."

Kyle sucked in a breath and arched a brow. He held the question back, unwilling to voice it in front of Michael. Had she kept him from balloon rides since Jordan's death? Would he have done the same if he'd been around?

She ignored his silent question and opened her door to get in the vehicle. He grabbed her elbow, steering her away from the minivan in a playful dance.

"Oh, no, you don't," he said.

"Yeah? Why's that?"

Pleasure ran through him at her teasing. "Okay, I admit that I need your help. Those two are going to be trouble— I can tell already."

Nikki smiled. "A guy like you? I'm not sure I buy that for one minute."

Kyle tried Michael's puppy-dog look on Nikki. No harm in trying. He begged with his eyes, copying Michael, both of them putting all their effort into persuading Nikki.

She burst out laughing. Kyle couldn't imagine a more pleasant sensation than the one swimming through him now at hearing her joyful laugh.

"Okay," she said. "Okay."

Michael jumped up and shouted. Kyle knew how he felt.

"Grab your jacket," Nikki said to him.

When he was out of earshot, Nikki leaned in. "I could throttle you right here, Kyle Morgan, for dragging us into this. I didn't want Michael in the balloon. I thought he could wait with Mark, worst case. But Mark is still not here."

"Then why do it?" He could kick himself.

"I can't resist the chance to see the look on those women's faces when I join you."

There was much more to it. Had to be. Nikki wouldn't sacrifice what she believed was best for Michael without good reason. Maybe her heart was just a little too soft when it came to Michael's pleading. Dare Kyle even think his own pleading had a thing to do with it? He could hope.

Regarding the reason she'd given for joining him, she wasn't the jealous type, and considering there wasn't anything of that nature between them, she had no reason to be. Kyle wouldn't add that he didn't think that would stop the women's flirting one bit unless Nikki gave them any indication that she and Kyle were a couple, and he wouldn't kid himself on that point. But her smile, and her gentle teasing, was a start toward restoring their friendship.

"About my note." He was crazy to bring it up, but it wasn't as if she could walk away now after assuring Michael they would ride in the balloon with Kyle.

When Michael returned, he held up the spaceship he'd put together. "Can I bring this?"

Good. Even if Nikki didn't answer him, the toy let him know she'd at least received the sack. Her mother hadn't trashed it.

"Sure," Kyle said and took Michael's hand. "Let's go."

Nikki locked her car and caught up with him, but she said nothing about his note. To Kyle's surprise, she slipped her hand into his. Was that her answer? Warmth spread through his chest. They strolled in comfortable silence toward the waiting passengers, and Kyle relished the feel of her warm, soft hand in his, the strength in her grip. For a sliver in time he could pretend that nothing had ever happened to rip their friendship apart. That Jordan was somewhere floating in his own balloon, with his own group.

But that wasn't the case, so Kyle settled for this moment, holding hands with Nikki. Her acceptance of him after everything was a balm to his battered soul.

When they approached the crew and the clients, he ignored the two women's questioning frowns and introduced Nikki and Michael.

"We paid for a private flight," the tall blonde said.

What was her name again? Donita? Kyle was terrible with names. He'd need to work on that if he was ever going to be as good at this as Nikki.

"Nikki owns the business, and this little boy is her nephew," he said, as if that settled the matter.

"Nice to meet you, ladies." She smiled, her comfortable way coaxing smiles from his two flirtatious clients. "I hope you don't mind if I join you this morning. I want to watch Kyle in action. I'm sure you can understand."

Their smiles lit up.

Oh, Nikki Alexander, you are a piece of work.

What am I doing? What am I doing?

Letting her emotions trump her better judgment, that was what. She held on to Michael, who whimpered as the balloon lifted higher and higher. The poor guy could barely see over the basket, but he could see enough. He'd wanted this, after all.

She couldn't believe she'd relented, given in to this after her resolve to turn Michael's thoughts and dreams in a completely different direction. Once Michael caught the fever, it would never let him go. She'd seen that firsthand with her father, then her brother and herself.

Then with Kyle.

She closed her eyes and listened to his animated voice as he spoke to his clients—sisters, Nikki had learned, named Cindy and Donita—talking them through the lift and answering their questions about the history of hot-air ballooning. Anything and everything.

He was a dream, really, and she couldn't blame the ladies for taking an interest in him as more than their pilot for the morning. With her eyes closed, Nikki could almost imagine her brother standing next to Kyle, and with that, she allowed herself to drift on the current of memories.

Kyle had come into their lives—hers and Jordan's—when she was in first grade, and Jordan and Kyle were in fourth. He and Jordan had quickly become best friends. As they grew older, they played a lot of nasty tricks on her—two scoundrel boys teasing the girl. After a time, they realized their antics didn't elicit the appropriate responses from her. Because Nikki had a schoolgirl crush on Kyle Morgan.

But she never let him know. No, she simply became part of their friendship—they became an inseparable three-some. That was, until Kyle and Jordan started taking risks that Nikki never would. Got involved in daredevil acts. First on their skateboards and then as they grew, with bigger things, like cars.

Kyle had almost been killed in a wreck. Jordan had been driving, no less. They fueled each other's need for an adrenaline rush, and in the end, Kyle had been the one to encourage Jordan to compete in the Gordon Bennett when the invitation came. Initially, Jordan had hesitated, only because it meant leaving Michael and traveling to Europe, where the race took place that year. But he wasn't new to leaving Michael for competitions, so in the end, he'd agreed.

Nikki rubbed her forehead. This wasn't where she wanted the memories to take her. She opened her eyes, welcoming the present. Her brother was gone, and she couldn't live in the past. The question she'd yet to answer, though, was could she live with Kyle reminding her of that past? Reminding her of the tragedy?

His dark hair whipped over his face with the slight breeze, the same breeze that carried the balloon envelope and the basket or gondola holding them. He smiled at something Cindy said and risked a glimpse Nikki's way, sneaking a quick wink.

Watching him in action, indeed.

He reached over and ruffled Michael's hair as he spoke, letting the boy know he hadn't been forgotten.

Yeah. A dream.

Nikki turned her back on Kyle and his clients, keeping a close hold on Michael in case he decided to do something reckless like climb up the side of the basket to get a better look.

Maybe it was also a dream that Nikki still had a school-girl crush on Kyle, even after the accident. Anger and resentment started again, deep in her stomach, but she pushed it down. She'd made the decision to forgive him. Asked God to help her follow through.

Kyle had asked for a chance, and she would give it. The investigation had said it was an accident. A tragic accident. Kyle couldn't be blamed for that, and yet she'd held him responsible anyway.

Wanting to forget, she squeezed Michael's hand, for once enjoying the sunrise without the added concern of piloting the balloon.

A hand from behind eased around her waist, startling her. "You okay?" Kyle whispered in her ear.

The guy was a flirt.

She closed her eyes, savoring the tenderness in his voice, his actions.

No. Kyle. I'm not okay. "Sure." She stepped away. "You handle everything like a pro, I might add."

Gentle laughter and clapping resounded from behind. Nikki glanced at Cindy and Donita, who were simply agreeing with her assessment of him. They turned away to enjoy the view, and maybe even to give her a little privacy with the pilot.

Nikki leaned closer. "I think you made some new friends."

"Really?" he asked. "'Cause I kind of hoped *you* wanted the job again."

His smile spread into that grin. Nikki suspected he knew full well how that affected women, but she turned away, unwilling to give in so easy. Let him suffer a little, though she smiled to herself while he couldn't see.

Kyle took her hint and struck up a conversation with Michael. In her nephew's voice, she heard the all-too-familiar thrill, and Nikki had let it happen. She'd agreed to let him on the ride.

When Jordan was alive, he'd taken his son up a few times, but small children were at a disadvantage and couldn't see that well from the basket anyway. Michael didn't remember much of his balloon rides with his father, and since Jordan's death, the tragedy had just been too much for all of them—and Michael hadn't been on a balloon since.

Until today.

Kyle had been back only two weeks and already he'd broken down the barriers she'd built to protect herself. Already she found herself thinking of him again, the way she had before. As someone she wanted in her life for much more than a friend. But was Nikki blinded by her long-harbored feelings for him? Was allowing him back in the right thing to do?

There was no doubt that if she hadn't been of age, her mother would absolutely forbid her to see him. Considering she lived with her mother, sought her approval just the same, what she thought happened to matter.

The morning drifted by and too soon the ride was over, the balloon crew assisting them all out of the basket after an uneventful landing. Nikki felt the sharp rush of anxiety she always felt when the basket touched the ground since Jordan's death. No one would ever know or see it on her face because she kept it hidden away, like some punishment or torment she deserved to experience. It kept her from forgetting Jordan and what had happened to him.

She assisted Kyle and his crew with deflating and folding the envelope and packing it and the gondola into the trailer, the whole time wishing for a moment alone with him. Wishing now she'd given him an answer instead of toying with his feelings. Though he smiled, she saw a shadow behind his eyes. Was that because of her?

Back at the warehouse, Cindy and Donita hung around talking to Kyle even after the crew had put away the balloon and equipment. Nikki thought they would never leave. She'd almost given up by the time the women drove from the parking lot. She leaned against her minivan, waiting for Kyle.

Michael rushed up to her, pointing his finger pistol to the ground as if it was locked and loaded. "Me and my posse are after the bad guys."

Nikki chuckled. He'd forgotten his toy spaceship quickly enough, putting it aside to pretend he was sheriff again. "You'd better hurry. I think they're getting away."

He ran around the other side of the minivan to duck behind the grille, shooting his imaginary gun at the make-believe outlaws.

Carrying a backpack, Kyle strolled to his vehicle and unlocked it as though he intended to leave without telling her goodbye. Without saying anything to Michael.

But that couldn't be true. Kyle wasn't like that.

He tossed in the bag and then turned, his eyes pinning hers as if he'd been aware of every second she'd watched him.

He grinned and headed her way.

"Thought they'd never leave," he said.

My sentiments, exactly.

Mark picked that moment to drive up and park, but Nikki wasn't about to let this chance pass.

"About your letter," she said.

Kyle froze, his smile wavering.

Nikki felt bad for dragging her answer out. She wished she could tell him everything rushing through her heart and mind, but Mark was climbing from his car.

"Sheriff Michael and I..." She cleared her throat.

"Yes?" He arched a brow and leaned in, his musky scent mixed with wind and clouds and desert air, wrapping around her.

"The sheriff and I, we don't want you to go. We want you to stay."

Kyle eased closer, too close for comfort, in fact. Nikki's breath caught. Mark's footfalls drew near.

"What about you, Nikki, just you. What do you want?"

Her mouth went dry. *What do I want?* "Thank you for your words in the letter. They meant the world to me. I want us to be friends again, like you said on the balloon today."

Friends. Just friends. That was all she could manage to say. He hadn't said he wanted anything more. But she was planning on leaving town, so why did it matter?

Chapter 8

Hearing her say the words, his heart jumped.

He couldn't exactly keep his promise to Jordan if Nikki didn't let him back in, ask him to stay. Say she wanted a friendship with him again, in spite of what stood between them. That was all he'd wanted in coming back—a chance.

Kyle swallowed hard.

But friends? Hearing that particular word, he realized with stunning clarity that he definitely wanted more than that with her. Maybe he'd walk through that door if it ever opened, but right now he wouldn't push it.

He chuckled. "It seems kind of strange, hearing you say that." Considering they'd grown up as close as any friends could get.

She tilted her head and studied him. Sadness flickered across her gaze. "I never wanted our friendship to end, Kyle."

He jammed his hands in his pockets and watched the cloud that had drifted in front of the sun. Mark didn't approach them but nodded as he opened the warehouse door, seeming to understand their conversation was private.

"But you're here now and for the moment," she said. "I'm here, too, so let's move forward. No need to look back."

Michael appeared by Nikki's side and tugged on her arm. "Can we go now? I'm hungry."

Nikki smiled down at Jordan's son. "Yes. We should get going."

The boy looked up at Kyle. "How about a picnic? Uncle Kyle can go with us."

An apologetic frown on her face, Nikki shook her head. "I'm sure Kyle has other plans, Michael. Maybe some other time."

She ruffled his hair and opened the door so he could climb into the minivan. She glanced back at Kyle. "I have to go check on Mom anyway."

"I would offer to go with you, but I'm not sure your mother is ready to accept me yet."

She stared at the pavement before looking at him. "I'm sorry about that. We'll just have to work on it, won't we?"

He nodded, squinting now as the sun moved from behind the clouds.

"See you later," she said, then she left his side to walk around and get into the minivan.

But Kyle didn't want it to end yet. Sweet moments were too hard to come by. With their schedules, when would he see her again other than coming and going? Would she continue to avoid him as she'd done the past couple of weeks despite her words today? He rushed around to catch her.

"Why don't you let me take Michael for a while," he offered.

Her responding frown didn't look promising. "That's not necessary."

Love in the Air

"I'm not talking about necessary. I'd love to spend time with him. He might even like some guy time." Kyle flashed a grin. "You know, man stuff for a change."

As though considering his offer, she glanced behind her at Michael, who was busy with his spaceship in the backseat. "I don't know."

Sensing her hesitation, he pressed on. "Just a couple of hours and I'll have him back at home, safe and sound."

Kyle cringed inside, thinking about the fact he hadn't exactly brought Jordan home safe and sound, but as she said, there was no need to look back. Time to move on.

Michael threw his arms over her seat. "Come on. I want to go with Uncle Kyle."

When she smiled, Kyle knew he had her.

"You don't have to do this, you know," she said.

"What are friends for?" He opened the back door, and Michael climbed out then bounced across the parking lot to Kyle's Denali. By spending time with Michael like this, he was also fulfilling the other part of his promise to Jordan. Finally, Nikki would let him.

"You're going to use that against me, aren't you?" she asked, a soft, teasing smile on her lips.

He leaned closer to the window, closer to her face. "Are you saying you don't want me to?"

And now he was flirting with Nikki. Really flirting with her. They were friends, yes, but there was a current of something more between them. Now if he could make sure that he didn't blow the friendship they had and lose her forever.

Her cheeks flushed a little, and she looked down as if she was shy. As if they hadn't known each other for years. When her eyes found his again, he held her gaze. It was all he could do not to lift his hand and cup her cheek. Feel her supple skin.

"Thank you for doing this. Michael needs this."

"So do I," he said and stepped away from the window.

She smiled, her face glowing with myriad emotions. Kyle would love to know everything she was thinking at that moment.

But Michael needed him now, so he turned his full attention to Jordan's son.

Nikki exited the parking lot, exhilarated by the turn of events.

She imagined little balloons floating around in her stomach, making her feel so lighthearted. There was something definitely different about Kyle since his return. She could easily fancy he looked at her differently, but that could also be her own wishful thinking. Wishful thinking that blurred her making the right decisions where Kyle was concerned.

In truth, they'd likely never be more than friends, and even with the way she'd always felt about him, she wasn't sure she could handle more than a friendship with him. She couldn't take more heartbreak that involved Kyle Morgan. The risk could be too great for not only her, but Michael and her mother.

Nikki sighed, hating that she could so easily douse the spark he'd kindled.

When she got home, she found her mother scrapbooking at the kitchen table. Well, that was an improvement from when she'd left earlier that morning. Her mother usually arose early, too, making coffee and breakfast. But this morning, she'd claimed she was too tired. Nikki knew it stemmed from her growing depressive state.

"Hey, Mom." Nikki looked over her mother's shoulder at the images of Jordan.

Maybe Nikki's initial assessment was wrong. Focusing

on Jordan right now was sure to drive her mother deeper into the dark place she chose to live these days. But maybe not. Maybe this was part of what had turned out to be a long grieving process. She wasn't sure a person could ever get over losing a child.

Mom used to manage the office and the business until Dad died. Then Jordan had taken over that responsibility. After that, her involvement in the family business was limited, and she came by the warehouse only on occasion. Sometimes she'd even help out on a balloon crew, but it became clear over time that Dad had been her reason to participate, and with him gone, she'd lost interest. Then she'd busied herself in a women's Bible-study group and some volunteer work. When Jordan was killed, she refused to step one foot into the warehouse. She dropped her other activities as well and stayed home after that, claiming she wanted to be there for Michael and Nikki.

Nikki effectively supported the three of them with the balloon business and her accounting work. Nikki gently placed her palm on Mom's shoulder, and her mother lifted her hand and squeezed Nikki's.

"I'm sorry you thought you needed to take Michael. Why didn't you just let him sleep? I would have gotten up for him. You know that." Her mother pushed from the chair, waving at her scrapbooking endeavors. "I'll have this cleaned up before din—"

Suddenly, she stiffened. "Where's Michael?"

This was the part Nikki hadn't exactly thought through that well when she'd agreed to allow Michael to go with Kyle. But there was no point in hiding that Nikki had found it in her heart to forgive him. Her mother would need to do that as well if she were ever to be herself again.

"He's with Kyle." There. She'd said it.

Her mother's swallow broke the momentary silence. "How could you trust him with Jordan's son like that?"

"Mom, we need to talk." She found her favorite comfy chair in the living room and prayed for the right words.

Her mother didn't follow but stood there, her eyes welling with tears. Nikki wondered if she'd made a mistake. Mom might not be ready to hear what she had to say. But if not now, then when?

"Please," she said.

Finally Mom sat across from her, but her face was drawn, lips pursed. "There's nothing you can say to convince me Kyle Morgan shouldn't be out of our lives for good."

God, give me the words.

"I blamed him, too. The race was his idea. But by all accounts, it's a safe sport. Jordan could have been killed in a car accident or any number of other ways, Mom. Blaming Kyle like this doesn't help anyone, especially not you."

"He could have persuaded him to land, avoid the storm. Something. And he just left him there to die alone."

Nikki got up and went to her mother, holding her while she sobbed.

"No," Nikki whispered. "He didn't leave him there to die alone. He was there with Jordan, who made him promise to help us and watch over us."

"I don't believe it," her mother said and tugged a tissue from a box on the side table. "Considering he didn't keep the promise. He left town."

"I should let you read the letter Kyle wrote me," Nikki said. "You have no reason to hold a grudge against him anymore. Even if he was guilty of all you say, he wants and needs forgiveness. And…I've missed him."

Her mother stood to face her now. "And even if all you say is true, there is no guarantee that he will not leave again, after he's gained your trust and much more, this time."

The woman left her standing there and went back to clean up the pictures of a young Jordan scattered on the table. Nikki followed her. Only then did Nikki notice Kyle had been cut from many of them. She fought her own need to break down and sob. When would this ever end?

This wasn't good for any of them, especially not Michael.

"You don't need to worry about me," Nikki said. "We're selling the business and starting a new life somewhere else, remember?"

Her mother didn't need to know that Kyle had offered to buy it. Nikki started feeling heartsick at everything. The conversation with her mother. Selling the business. And the prospect of Kyle walking out on them again. She hated the seed her mother had planted.

Someone knocked on the door. "That must be Kyle with Michael now," she said.

Kyle hadn't lasted long in Michael's company. Making her way to the door, she drew in a breath to tease him. She opened the door.

"Mark?" Surprise and disappointment mingled in her chest. "What are you doing here?"

Nikki glanced behind her and stepped outside.

"I'm sorry to stop by your house," he said. "But I wanted a chance to talk to you alone."

She shook her head, a little confused.

"At the warehouse, Kyle might walk in. Like I said, I wanted to talk to you in private, if that's okay." He laughed nervously.

"What's wrong with Kyle hearing?" Nikki clicked the door completely shut and held up her finger. "Hold that thought. Let me grab my purse. We can talk over a cup of coffee at the Waffle House on the corner."

Five minutes later, she and Mark sat at a booth and ordered coffee. She watched her cell phone so she wouldn't miss Kyle's call when he was ready to deliver Michael. She'd texted him to call her first. The last thing she wanted was for him to deliver Michael home and face her mother when she wasn't there.

"So tell me what's on your mind." She kept the fear from her tone, but she hoped Mark wasn't going to malign Kyle the way her mother had. "Why the secrecy?"

"I apologize for the dramatics. It's not really a secret—it's just that I wanted a chance to talk to you about this alone, without input from Kyle."

"Okay?"

"You've decided to sell the business, and I should be out looking for another job. I know that. But I knew your father, and I want you to get your money's worth."

"I appreciate that."

"I think you should enter the competition at the fiesta." The room tilted a little. "Mark, I—"

"Just hear me out. I understand the reasons why you haven't before. The American Challenge is a long-distance gas-balloon race like the Gordon Bennett in which your brother was killed. But you want me to build this business up again, and to do that we need to get our name in the papers. Make your father's business shine again before you bow out altogether."

Nikki sat stunned, considering Mark's words. "I was thinking we'll be pretty busy just offering rides during the season. Plus, haven't we missed the deadline for entering?"

"I've already taken care of that, if you'll agree. I know I haven't been in this circle for long, but I've met people who can pull strings, and everyone respected your father.

And your brother. Let's just say, people want to see you back full force."

"Sounds like you've been scheming behind my back," she said, though she laced her words with warmth. She knew Mark meant well.

But he just didn't understand how deep the pain went. How could he?

A waitress set cups before them and poured hot, steaming coffee. "Cream and sugar?"

Though she asked the question, she didn't wait for an answer as she set a small bowl of individual packets of sugar and sugar-free sweeteners, and minicartons of half-and-half down on the table.

Mark fixed his coffee the way he liked and took a sip before he turned his attention back to Nikki. "It's your decision," he said. "Just trying to help."

"And you didn't want Kyle to hear about this why?"

"I wanted a chance to hear your thoughts first."

"You think he would talk me into doing something I don't feel right about? Is that it?"

Mark quirked a smile. "Your relationship with him is your business. I can't say which way he will fall on this."

She looked down into her cup of coffee. "I appreciate everything you've done. I need to give it some thought and prayer. I'll tell you my first reaction when you brought it up was no. After everything we've been through, competing is the last thing I want to do. But I'm trying to get past this. And then there's Mom. She won't be happy."

"So let Kyle compete instead. There's a place for one of you."

"What about the new guy, Chase?"

Mark took another sip of coffee. "I think he'll work best where I have him, an extra pilot to offer rides as we build back up. So, Kyle, then?"

"No, I think if it happens, I want to be the one." Nikki couldn't explain her feelings on that point, but it felt right to say the words.

Her phone buzzed, and she looked down at the text. "Speaking of Kyle, he has Michael, and I need to go meet him."

Mark leaned in close. "I know I said it wasn't my business, but I care about you, Michael and your mother. Kyle seems like a nice enough guy, but I get the sense he's not completely aboveboard."

"Aboveboard?"

"He's hiding something."

Chapter 9

Nikki met Kyle at home just as he turned in to the driveway. True to his word, he'd kept Michael for only a couple of hours.

His broad grin in place, Kyle crossed his arms and leaned against the Denali. Was he expecting her to invite him in?

She might have considered it, but Mark's suggestion that she compete in the gas-balloon race and his warning about Kyle both weighed heavy on her heart. She doubted she would be good company this afternoon. Kyle would see right through her.

As he studied her, his lively smile wavered. "What's wrong?"

Yep. Right through her.

Nikki waved him off with a scoff, pretending his question was ridiculous. "Oh, nothing. I'm just tired."

"Yeah, right." Kyle shoved away from his vehicle but remained standing in the same spot. "How's your mom?"

Nikki smiled at that. "So you're just going to keep probing until you find the source of my distress?"

"Pretty much, yeah." His smile had now flattened to a half grin.

"Well, you can stop worrying." Nikki stretched and yawned. "I'm going to take a nap now."

Though he never quite lost the smile, disappointment flickered in his gaze. "Okay. See you around."

Nikki shared his disappointment. She didn't want to see him go, but she needed time alone to think. His leaving now, as if she'd hurt him, added to her heavy mood.

He climbed into the Denali, and just before he backed out, he winked at her. And with that, some of the guilt eased up. He wasn't hurt—not really. He understood her.

There wasn't anyone who knew her better than this man.

Oh, Lord, what am I going to do?

The guy was too much for her to resist. She didn't think she'd ever get over him if it came to that. Heading back inside, Nikki decided to follow through with what she'd told Kyle. Mom baked a cake and Nikki rested on the sofa while Michael watched an old animated movie. While rodents floated in a matchbox attached to helium balloons, Nikki thought about her conversation with Mark.

Kyle probably had a few things he hadn't told Nikki, sure. Who didn't have a few secrets? She brushed aside Mark's warning for now, figuring he was overly concerned for Nikki. He didn't know Kyle the way she did. As for the gas-balloon race, Nikki was surprised that she was beginning to warm to the idea.

Sunday was filled with church and laundry. Kyle had piloted the one balloon ride that evening. On Monday Nikki sat up on her bed, almost grateful for the rain because that meant the balloon rides were canceled for the day. This morning she had an important interview. The cell phone cradled in her hand, she waited for the call.

God, I really want this job.

At the silent prayer, a deep sadness squeezed her chest. Of course she wanted it, didn't she? Getting the job would mean a move to Tulsa, but that was what she'd been aiming for—a complete break from her life here in New Mexico. And if she didn't have a buyer for Sky High by then, Mark could handle that end of things. Mark and Kyle.

She'd considered the change for weeks before taking the idea seriously and then had sent her résumé out to test the waters, as it were. Made the decision, after discussing it with Mom, of course, to sell the business.

Then, in walked Kyle Morgan.

That he'd stepped back into her life shouldn't make a difference. Nikki squeezed her temples, feeling the tension building.

Over the past couple of weeks, Nikki had been excited that she was beginning to get a few responses to her résumé. A couple of the phone interviews didn't go any further, but then a friend, Tina, recommended Nikki to her brother, Jeff, who needed someone with her talents in his company—an energy company in Tulsa. He would call in fifteen minutes.

Fifteen minutes could decide her future. Hers, Mom's and Michael's. But Nikki was beyond torn. Her schoolgirl crush on Kyle had morphed into something much more, and it was giving her fits. She couldn't smash it, douse it or bury it, no matter how hard she tried.

And lately, she had the sneaking feeling Kyle might even be cracking through the walnut shell of her mother's heart. A knot swelled in her throat. Bad timing. She needed to sound professional and articulate for the call.

She was torn about the future. Each day spent in Kyle's company made her that much more vulnerable to him.

But how could she stake her life, her future—Michael's future—on Kyle, the man who'd left them three years ago without so much as a goodbye?

If only she didn't see such a difference in him now, as though he was actually interested in her, returned her not-so-platonic feelings. Nikki struggled to believe it could be possible, considering she'd grown up with the guy. She'd think he would have noticed her in that way before now. He would have given her a sign, expressed his interest, something.

Michael came running into the bedroom, flying an airplane. He ran back out, the plastic toy floating on imaginary clouds by his side. School was out today for a teacher workday, another reason for which she could thank God for the rain, which kept her at home. The only downside was the financial ramifications.

The phone rang and Nikki jumped. She had another ten minutes. She wasn't ready yet.

When she looked at the caller ID she saw it was Kyle. *Not now, Kyle.* Chewing her lip, she declined the call. She'd call him back afterward, except then she might end up telling him about her interview. Why should she hesitate, though? Telling him, keeping him informed of her plans, was the right thing to do. Kyle and Mark could handle things if she ended up moving before selling.

He'd offered at one point to buy it from her, but she couldn't handle the thought of it. Besides, she wasn't sure he was serious. Nikki lost track of time with her thoughts, and the cell rang again. Her heart zip-lined.

She mustered her most warm and professional tone and answered. A half hour later, she ended the call, a smile on her lips and a thrill shooting through her. After spending her whole life in the balloon business, she wasn't sure it would be possible to do something else with her life, giving up the balloon business completely. But she'd made the first step.

Hopping from the bed, she flung the door open to tell her mother, when laughter accosted her from the living room.

Nikki stepped from the hallway and startled.

Kyle held Michael in the air, flying him around, much as her nephew had done the small toy plane. Warmth spreading through her heart, she leaned against the doorjamb, absorbing the scene.

Wasn't this just what she'd wanted for Michael—a father figure? If it couldn't be Jordan, then who better than Uncle Kyle? The question caught her off guard. Tears surged and she swiped at them before someone noticed. Then she caught sight of Mom opposite her, looking on with a soft smile playing across her features.

Kyle had found his way back into all their hearts.

Nikki wasn't sure he'd ever been gone from hers, and with the look on Mom's face, Nikki knew the woman had all but forgiven Kyle, too. They'd needed someone to blame for Jordan's death, and shame on them for blaming Kyle.

He couldn't have known where things would take any of them. Just as Nikki couldn't know where her decision to move on in a physical, permanent way would take them, either.

Kyle brought Michael in for a landing on his feet and then turned his focus on Nikki as if he'd been completely aware of her from the moment she'd stepped into the room. How did he do that?

"Hey, there." He ran his hand over his mouth, a familiar mannerism that told her he was unsure of himself.

Adorable. Irresistible. "Hey, there, yourself," she said and stepped forward.

"I tried to call."

"I was on the phone, sorry."

He studied her. Should she tell him?

"So—" he cleared his throat "—I'm sorry to drop by unannounced. I thought we could go do something together. All of us."

He glanced at her mother.

"You guys go on without me." Mom waved her hand and turned her back, but not before Nikki saw the moisture in her eyes.

Nikki looked down and realized she was in her oversize sweats, socks and tacky T-shirt, her hair a tangled mess pinned to the top of her head. She gasped and pressed her hands to her head. As if that was going to help. "I must look a mess."

The grin Kyle gave her sent heat to her knees. "I don't know. I think you're kind of cute," he said. "I've always been a big fan of the natural look."

"You." Nikki grabbed a throw pillow from a chair and tossed it at him, laughing. "What did you have in mind?"

"I don't care," he said. Hesitating, his eyes searched hers. "As long as we can spend the day together. You decide."

What am I going to do?

He'd never enjoyed a rainy day so much.

Kyle steered his bumper car into Nikki's, and Michael bumped her on the other side, pinning her in the corner. She threw her head back in laughter, joining Kyle's own outburst and Michael's giggles. Screams and laughter from the patrons accompanied the loud music playing over the stereo and little flashes of electricity where the car's tail met the ceiling.

Nikki found her escape and took it, whizzing around and into the other bumper cars and ramming Kyle. He steered and bumped and swerved and someone collided with him from behind, and so it continued until their time in the cars came to an end. Kyle stumbled from his and Michael climbed out, grinning from ear to ear and laughing at Kyle.

Nikki grabbed Michael's hand and they exited the bumper-car area to face their next challenge in the indoor amusement facility. Kyle jammed his hands into his pockets, fighting the urge to grab on to Nikki's, making them a threesome—a family. He reminded himself they were far from that.

"What next?" Kyle asked.

Nikki glanced at her watch. Disappointment taunted him. He'd hoped she was having a good time, too. Her smile answered him in a way that words couldn't, and he relaxed.

"Can we get cotton candy?" Michael pointed to the food vendor stand.

"Oh, no, you've had enough junk for one day." She shoved her gorgeous tresses over her shoulders and looked around the facility.

She'd transformed from the sweats and T-shirt into a dazzling turquoise shirt with tiny sparkles across the pattern on the front and formfitting jeans. Her massive black mane hung free below her shoulders, and she wore a hint of blush on her cheeks. A smidgen of glossy pink on her lips.

The girl dazzled him. Had she dressed up just for him? The thought made him dizzy. When he realized he was staring, he pulled his gaze away.

"Want to try rock-climbing?" Kyle asked, clearing his throat.

A young boy ran into him in his escape from his playful friends, and Kyle steered the boy back to his mom, who chased him.

"I'm hungry," Michael whined.

"You sure you're not ready to be free from us? We've been at it all day," Nikki said.

"Are you kidding? I could keep going like this for a few more hours, at least," he said. "But if it means you'll stick with me a little longer, we can do something…um…"

"Boring?" She arched a brow. "You were going to say *boring.*"

"Was not," he teased. "I was going to say *leisurely.*"

Smiling, Nikki gave him a friendly punch on the arm. "I'm just not accustomed to your pace. I'm surprised Michael isn't tired already, but I'm glad he'll sleep well tonight."

Though he'd dreaded looking, he was the one to glance at his watch this time. "No wonder Michael's hungry. It's almost six."

He'd normally be hungry himself, but hanging around Nikki had given him a kind of nervous energy, and he was too wound up to think about food. That was a first for him, and so was today—just being with her in a non-work-related capacity—at least since his return. The way they used to do when Jordan was alive.

He didn't want this to end yet, but how did Nikki feel?

Nikki watched him as if she was considering ending their time together, though he could see she wavered.

"I have an idea," he said. "I have a great view of the sunset from my apartment balcony. Let's go back there, and I'll cook dinner for us."

"It's raining. How are we going to see the sunset?" she asked.

"The clouds have probably cleared out by now, or they will be by then. I'm optimistic, what can I say."

"You sure? That's a lot of trouble." She tilted her head

to the side, and her hair fell away from her face. He loved
it when she did that.

"I'm being selfish. I can't remember the last time I've
had so much fun. Can you blame me if I don't want it to
end?"

"I've had a great time today, too, Kyle." She hung her
head again then glanced back up at him. "This has been
really good for Michael."

She rubbed her hand over the boy's head. Annoyed,
Michael shifted away from her, his attention glued to the
busy arcade across the way.

It's been good for me, too. But Kyle kept those words to
himself. He wanted to be more than friends with her, and
he thought something was happening between them but
didn't know if Nikki felt it, too. Sure, he knew she'd had a
crush on him before, but they'd been kids, and he figured
by now she'd grown out of that. Moved on, especially in
light of everything that had happened.

Kyle tugged his hand from his pocket and held it out
for Nikki, hoping she'd take it much the way she'd done
that Saturday they'd taken his clients, Cindy and Donita,
up in the balloon. "Will you come over, then? Let me cook
for you?"

A tender smile lifted the corners of her pinkish lips.
Beautiful lips.

"I'd like that."

When Nikki placed her hand in his, his heart floated on
a blanket of warmth. Soaring thousands of feet from the
earth in a hot-air balloon had nothing on this.

Three hours later, Michael had conked out on the sofa,
having eaten more than his share of the tacos Kyle had
made for them. He couldn't have planned this better if
he had tried.

He and Nikki sat on the balcony in wicker chairs,

though Nikki's was a love seat, their feet propped on the small matching coffee table. They'd missed the sunset because the clouds hadn't moved out as Kyle had hoped, but he and Nikki weren't strangers to watching the sunset on their balloon rides.

A soft, cool breeze lifted her hair, and she wrapped her arms around herself under the blanket he'd offered. The comfortable silence between them kept him warm enough.

They'd spent the evening reminiscing about their lives growing up with Jordan. Kyle savored the fact he heard no bitterness or resentment toward him in her tone—nothing like that day when he'd first seen her in the warehouse. With that, he could believe she'd let go of what she'd held against him.

Closing her eyes, she rested her head against the seatback and sighed. Only one thing could make Kyle more content at the moment—he wanted to sit next to her on the small sofa—the love seat—and snuggle. Wrap his arms around her. Keep her warm.

When Kyle had promised Jordan he would watch out for Nikki, he had no idea he could want so much more than that. To be more to her than a longtime friend. And he wanted to know her much better than he already knew her.

I'm falling for her.

"I know Jordan would be proud of how good you are with his son," he said.

Her eyes fluttered open then. Had she fallen asleep? Kyle had woken her with his words.

"I don't feel like I'm being good to him at the moment since I left him sleeping on your couch." She stretched and yawned. "We should get going."

She rose from the love seat and folded the blanket.

He'd ruined everything. "I wish you didn't have to."

Nikki moved toward him and pressed the blanket into

his arms, her eyes locking with his. "Me either," she whispered.

Her words ignited something in him. His breath caught. She turned to leave, and he grabbed her hand, stopping her. Nikki stared at the ground, but her fingers laced with his. He tossed the blanket down and gently urged her toward him, though not all the way into his arms.

Angling her head, she looked at his arms, his chest, anything but his face. "Kyle." She whispered his name again and drew in a breath—

He lifted his hand to her cheek, silencing her next words. He wasn't about to let her finish. He couldn't risk it. He tilted her chin up, and her eyes followed, her lashes fluttering. Shy, Nikki stood before him, expectant.

They'd never crossed this line, and he prayed, oh, how he prayed, that he wasn't about to ruin everything with her. When Nikki didn't pull away, he took that as permission and leaned near, his face an inch from hers. Her chest rose and fell with her breath. He wanted to linger there forever, breathing in the essence that was Nikki. He'd known her for most of his life, but never like this.

Slowly, he eased forward and put his lips on hers, softly, gently. Her sweet response was all the encouragement he needed, and he drew her closer, folding his arms around her, pressing her softness against him.

Then he ended the kiss, a big first for them. He feared it would be a last, too.

Not wanting the moment to end, he hugged her to him and played with the long tresses hanging down her back. Only now did he realize he'd ever had thoughts of kissing Nikki. He realized just how deep he'd buried his attraction to her for Jordan's sake. For the sake of keeping the precious friendship he had with Jordan and Nikki intact.

And now had he let himself slip and ruined what little they had in the way of a new beginning?

She eased from his arms, and though her face reflected a light he hadn't seen before, a frown also worried her brows.

Please tell me I didn't just ruin everything. Maybe it wasn't too late. Maybe he could salvage things. Kyle stepped back. "I'm sorry.... I...shouldn't have done that."

Chapter 10

Nikki pressed her fingers over her lips. She could hardly believe they'd just shared a kiss. For so long she'd wanted him to notice her, and to kiss her—it was a dream. But a dream from too many years gone by. Too many obstacles stood between them in her mind. In her heart.

And now he was apologizing? Did he really regret it? Hurt and uncertainty rained down on her. She wanted to tell him that she'd wanted the kiss, too. That it wasn't his fault.

His expression turned more somber, searching. "I'm serious. I wouldn't ruin what we've had together for anything. If I shouldn't have kissed you…I'm…sorry. But I need to know how you feel."

So many emotions battled for her attention at the moment, and her heart danced to an unfamiliar rhythm. "I think you already know, but I can't…"

"Go on," he said, his voice twisting with anguish.

"I can't tell you that you didn't just ruin everything.

That *we* didn't ruin our friendship." Just beyond the sliding glass door, Michael stirred on the couch. "I mean, if you decide, if *we* decide we want to explore a new kind of friendship, something more between us—" heat flooded her cheeks "—I don't know where it will lead. And then where will that leave us? Where will that leave Michael? So maybe we shouldn't even go there. He's already lost enough."

She couldn't bear it if she lost Kyle again due to her own selfish desires. He'd left once before when she'd needed him. Nikki wasn't too sure she could count on him to stick around.

Kyle drew in a long breath, his expression thoughtful and tender. Her heart jumped. She longed to ask him how he really felt about her, too. Would he just play with her for a while and then toss her aside the way she'd seen so many guys do?

"I can understand that you don't want him to lose someone else." Kyle took a step closer, as if they weren't close enough.

For so long Nikki had wanted Kyle's attention. Wanted to date him, be his girlfriend, wanted to be the object of his affection, of his love. But never had she expected the pure terror that would course through her if he ever kissed her.

"Good." *I'm afraid of losing you, too.* What a coward she'd become.

"Nikki—" his voice cracked "—don't you know how much you mean to me by now? You and Michael both. All I'm asking is for a chance."

Nikki's heart twisted.

Kyle took her hand in his. "I promise you, if something happens to end things between us, it will be your choice, not mine."

"How can you promise me so much so soon?" she said. "It was only one kiss."

But even one kiss between the two of them meant so much more.

Letting go of her hand, he stepped back as if she'd slapped him, hurt in his eyes. Nikki couldn't stand it.

She sighed, feeling herself sinking to the hard cold ground much too fast. This was going to hurt. "I'm not ready for Michael to get the wrong idea. We need to take our time, Kyle, see if…" What? They'd end up a permanent couple?

The room swam a little, and Nikki reached for a chair.

Kyle swept her off her feet and planted her on the love seat again. "Are you okay?"

A small laugh escaped. "I don't know what's the matter with me." *Yes, I do.*

Kyle pressed his hand over her forehead. "No fever that I can tell. You sure you're all right?"

Kyle's furrowed brow almost made her laugh again. How could she tell him she was dizzy with his affection? That her schoolgirl crush had found traction. Fear gripped her heart. This was Kyle—the man she'd spent the past three years blaming for her brother's death. She'd forgiven him for that, yes, but she still struggled with the way he'd left them.

And forgiving someone was one thing. Sharing her heart and maybe a lifelong commitment was another.

"I'm fine, and we really need to get home." Before either of them did something or said something more they might regret tomorrow.

A movement behind the sliding glass door drew her attention. Michael sat up now and rubbed his eyes. She didn't have much time.

Nikki stood slowly, and Kyle didn't step away. "Look,

Kyle...there's something you should know," she said, lifting her eyes to his clear blue ones.

The clouds had finally parted, and the moon shone down on them.

"I'm listening."

The way he looked at her made it more difficult to tell him this. "Remember today when you called and I told you later that I was on the phone?"

"Yes."

"I was on an interview for a position in Tulsa. It looks promising." There. She'd gotten that off her chest.

Kyle crossed the balcony and leaned against the railing, putting a big, gaping hole between them. Or had she been the one? He gazed up at the stars, only now coming out from behind the clouds, looking for all the world like a guy who knew he'd lost an important race.

"I just wanted you to know everything." And with her words, other words floated across her thoughts.

He's hiding something.

Mark's warning came back to her. Now? She had to think of that now?

Before they even took one more step into their possible future together, she needed to know. "And what I need to hear from you is if there's anything you've been hiding from me. Anything you want to tell me."

The problem was, she still had one more thing to tell him.

That I love you?

Kyle swallowed. He could hardly wrap his mind around those words. He frowned, suddenly as afraid as she appeared.

Clearly, Nikki wasn't ready to hear those words, either. He offered a grin instead. "All in good time." The thing was, it sounded as if he didn't have a lot of time. Sure, he could follow her there if she ended up leaving. He'd just go with her—but he couldn't exactly do that if their relationship wasn't solid.

Michael hugged him. Kyle hadn't even noticed his approach. He reached down and lifted the boy into his arms and squeezed. "Come on, little buddy. Let's get you home."

He winced inside, wondering if Michael would chide him for not calling him Sheriff, but the boy settled into his arms, tired from a day of fun. Kyle hoped they could share more of them as he carried the boy out to his Denali and buckled him in.

On the drive home, Nikki remained silent, and this time it wasn't the comfortable silence they'd shared on his balcony. It was a painful silence that was filled with fear and regret and tension. They'd not had that kind of apprehension between them since immediately after Jordan's death, and he could only believe that was the cause. Would that always stand between them?

He carried Michael into the house for her and put the boy gently in his bed. While Nikki tucked him in, Kyle watched from the door, wishing that this could be his family.

Would Jordan have approved? When she'd finished, and Michael rolled over and snuggled deeper into the covers and pillows, she glanced up, a soft smile playing on her lips.

Leaving the door cracked, Nikki led Kyle down the hallway and out the front door. "Thank you for today."

While he wanted to kiss her again, so he'd know it hadn't been a dream, her warning had been clear. Well, more like fair to partly cloudy, and unless the weather was clear, there wouldn't be any flying.

She wanted to take things slowly. Still, he couldn't help

feel the tinge of excitement burst through the caution she'd left him. This was really happening between them, although he felt like a balloonist in unfamiliar territory, struggling to maneuver over power lines.

For balloonists, there was almost nothing more dangerous, more deadly, than hitting a power line. Kyle had experienced something more deadly, and the reminder dampened his spirits. He stared at the porch to compose his emotions before looking back up at Nikki.

She watched him, waiting. Was she reading his distress? He hoped not.

He wanted to lift her soft hand to his lips, feel her skin, but instead, he jammed his hands in his pockets. The way he felt about her now was definitely unfamiliar territory.

"So you think you might have a job in Tulsa. And you're selling your business…" What exactly was he trying to say?

She'd left him a little confused about what she wanted. If there was something between them, something that she wanted to happen, then her starting a new life somewhere else wouldn't keep him away. It wouldn't keep them apart.

Unless she wanted it to. Unless leaving him behind was part of the starting-a-new-life package. Add to that, he loved flying balloons and he knew she did, as well. How could she give up what she had here?

"Slow down," she said. "I just wanted to be honest with you. I didn't want you to be blindsided by any of it."

"I see." Boy, did he sound desperate. He'd never felt so out of control, either.

Oh, yes, you have.

Nikki smiled softy, breaking through his unsettled thoughts. For a brief moment, he saw her as a young girl again, laughing and smiling and whirling on the steps to wave goodbye.

When she disappeared inside the house, he pulled his cell from his pocket and walked back to the Denali.

Kerry Carnes, his contact for the Gordon Bennett. She was the team liaison.

Nikki's question rushed back to him: *Is there anything you've been hiding from me?*

Oh, Lord, how do I tell her?

He couldn't tell her. Not yet. Not when they were only beginning to explore something more than a friendship. That news would completely kill anything he might have with her. And he treasured their friendship so much—was this all a mistake?

Jordan shouldn't have extracted such a promise from him, but that was one last promise Kyle intended to keep. If only he could find a way to tell Nikki. Make her understand.

Maybe in the end, it would have been better for Nikki, for Michael, if Kyle hadn't stepped back into their lives.

Alone in her room, Nikki closed her eyes and remembered the kiss. Kyle's kiss might have been everything she could have wanted if it weren't for the tragedy that tainted their past.

She opened the bottom drawer in her dresser and pulled out an old photo album. Flipping open to the first set of images—photographs pressed against an adhesive then covered in a transparent, protective sheet—Nikki pressed her fingers to the images staring back at her.

Tears flowed freely. So many times she'd wanted to leaf through the photographs and remember Jordan. Remember Kyle. Think on their times together.

But thoughts of looking at the photographs, of facing all they'd lost, was too painful. Looking at them now, she admitted it was still much more painful than she would have thought, or than she wanted to experience. Still, she needed to process through everything.

She couldn't hope to give her and Kyle a chance if she didn't work through things. Her family had lost so much already. Moving past this, exploring what she'd always felt for Kyle. Now that he apparently returned those feelings might mean losing even more.

But Nikki pressed forward, remembering each moment the pictures captured.

The three of them at an amusement park one summer with the other church kids. They didn't need more amusement than the hot-air balloons that were so much a part of their daily lives, but they'd gone along with the church group for the experience.

Jordan's antics always ended up getting Kyle in trouble. Her brother was such a head-turner. Kyle, too, with his dimpled smile.

The feeling of her heart racing in her chest at that moment when he'd flashed her that grin and winked at her—oblivious to how he affected her—was fresh in her heart and mind. She'd taken the picture to hide her blush.

Nikki laughed to herself and pressed her cheek against her palm, looking at the pictures. Who would have thought he could feel the same way. Problem was, she wasn't sure if he did feel the same way. Had he kissed her, had everything been about some weird sense of making amends? Making up for his part in Jordan's death?

Making up for the fact that he'd survived and Jordan hadn't?

Nikki flipped the album closed and tucked it back in the drawer, safely underneath a few articles of clothing. She wiped at her eyes and blew her nose. Somehow she would have to get past her thoughts always returning to that morbid and dark place.

She wasn't sure she could ever be with Kyle and keep her mind from lingering in the shadows of their past.

Chapter 11

Kyle tossed and turned that night, his mind unable to let go long enough to fall asleep.

Images of Nikki's beautiful face, the feel of her kiss, gave way to Jordan's pleading eyes before he died, until finally Kyle drifted into a fitful sleep, and memories he'd hidden or buried burst onto the landscape of his dreams.

Jordan's face grew more determined. "We're ahead of the storm," he said. "Not like we're going to get another chance like this. We have to win."

Kyle argued with him, realizing now the danger they were in. "We're risking too much. What about your sister? Your mother? Your son, Jordan? What if this doesn't end well? We need to land."

"We're staying. We're going to win."

The wind surged ahead of the storm clouds and captured their gas balloon and wouldn't let go, pushing them too hard and fast.

Off course.

The balloon began deflating, collapsing. Jordan worked to keep the balloon inflated, to find the right altitude to take them ahead of the storm.

They'd lost altitude rapidly, and the Mediterranean Sea would soon give way to the coastline of Italy. "We should jump while we're over water—that way we at least have a chance of survival. We can't survive if we hit the ground at this height."

By the time Jordan agreed, it was almost too late.

"NO...!"

When Kyle woke, he was sitting up, covered in sweat. His own voice rang in his ears. Had he woken up the neighbors through the thin walls of his apartment? He lay there for a few moments and stared at the ceiling, afraid to fall asleep again.

Instead of risking it, he got up and went to the bathroom to splash water on his face. When he stared at the mirror, he saw Jordan's face.

What am I doing?

When he got back in bed, he flipped on the nightstand lamp and dug around in the drawer until he found his Bible. He hadn't opened the pages in far too long, but now was as good a time as any to start reading again. Maybe that would put his mind to rest, and he could sleep without the nightmares.

What was he doing wooing the sister of his best friend, who'd kept them apart before he'd died? Kyle believed she was over what had happened and no longer blamed him, but as guilt snaked around his heart, he realized he hadn't forgiven himself.

He blamed himself for everything that had happened, but especially for leaving Nikki and Michael when they needed him the most. He'd been too weak in character to look them in the eyes.

Kyle bowed his head and prayed, allowing his heart to cry out to God, to finally hand over what was there all along. What he'd tried to ignore. Act as if it didn't matter, as if it wasn't eating away at him every day.

Please help me to let go of blaming myself. Of the guilt for my part in hurting Nikki and Michael. Help me to be a better man. And please, if we shouldn't be together, if I would only hurt her again, put a stop to this. I don't ever want to hurt her again.

On Tuesday, Kyle slept in a little because his wedding balloon flight had been canceled. The couple had gotten stuck in the Caribbean due to a hurricane. Just as well because he had to catch up on one of his contract programming projects for a bank.

Kyle hadn't heard back from Kerry Carnes but figured she hadn't had a chance to call him back. He'd try her again.

He reached her on the first ring this time. "Kerry, this is Kyle Morgan."

His gut churned over the whole thing, but he was determined to keep this last promise to Jordan. He just didn't know if Jordan would expect him to, and he didn't like to think of Nikki's reaction. He frowned and waited for Kerry's reply.

"We've lost one of your team members. Bradley Hanes has pulled out. You don't need three, of course. It could just be you and Taylor, but if you want three people manning the balloon, we need to discuss who you feel comfortable flying with. I learned that Nikki Alexander is on a team in the American Challenge. If you agree, I'm sure I could get quick approval, if she's willing, of course."

Nikki Alexander is on a team in the American Challenge...

Kyle's heart flatlined.

"What did you say?" Surely she was mistaken.

"Jordan Alexander's sister. Maybe she could join your team for the Gordon Bennett."

Kyle couldn't respond.

"Kyle? You there?"

"I'm here."

"Look, maybe I'm being insensitive, considering how her brother died. But I figured since you're competing…"

"No. Find someone else."

"We're kind of running out of time. Got any suggestions?"

"Give me some time to think about it." Maybe he and Taylor would be better off just the two of them.

"Let me know by the end of the day." Kerry drew in a breath and hesitated. "Everything okay, Kyle? You still want to compete, don't you?"

Why would she ask that?

"Of course I do." No matter his trepidation, he couldn't imagine passing up on the opportunity. "I'll call you back later, then."

Kyle splashed more water on his face in the bathroom. He was doing that a lot lately. He stared at the mirror again. At his eyes, bloodshot from lack of sleep. "Oh, Nikki, you are so not competing in the American Challenge."

Nikki took Michael to school instead of letting him ride the bus. A blustery day, the weather wasn't cooperating and her balloon ride was canceled. She pulled in front of the school behind a long line of cars and school buses.

Backpack in place, Michael opened the door but hung back. "When can we see Uncle Kyle again?"

Oh, boy. Michael was already too attached to the man. Admittedly, so was Nikki, and having a great time on

Monday had only made things worse. Or better, depending on one's perspective.

She reached over and rustled his hair. "I don't know, sweetie. Soon, probably."

"This afternoon? After school? Maybe Grandma can ask him over for spaghetti night."

Nikki laughed. "You'd better get to class. We'll see what can be arranged."

After dropping Michael off, Nikki prayed he'd have another good day and wouldn't run into that bully again. The principal had shown mercy to Michael and the bully, Timmy Reed. Regardless, Nikki had given Michael permission to defend himself again if he had to. She just hoped it wouldn't come to that.

Before settling in to spend time on a client's books, she ran a few errands, including picking up some medication the doctor had prescribed for Mom. Thank goodness she'd finally agreed to get counseling in addition to seeing a doctor to discuss her struggle with depression.

Nikki wasn't so sure she didn't need Christian counseling herself, another perspective on how to view everything going on in her life. She still hadn't told her mother she had agreed to fly in the American Challenge. Once her mother had a few good days, then Nikki would tell her the news.

How in the world was she going to tell her? She wanted to share the news with her in enough time that she could back out if she had to and they could get someone else to take her place. But Mark had convinced her entering the race, flying on an already assembled team, made sense.

The American Challenge was a gas-balloon race that measured distance, so she might be in the air over a two- or three-day period. It wasn't as if she could keep that from her mother.

Or Kyle.

Sky High didn't own a gas balloon anymore, either. Jordan and Kyle had used it when they'd raced the American Challenge, and she'd sold it after Jordan died—though he'd been in another balloon, sponsored by a new and upcoming experimental-balloon company, during the race in which he'd died. That balloon had been destroyed, of course.

Regardless of whose balloon she piloted, the fact she was one of the pilots would be good enough to put her balloon company—Dad's company—back on the proverbial map. Then she'd get the offer she wanted for the business—or at least Mark seemed to think so.

She turned the corner onto the street that would take her to the Sky High warehouse. She couldn't begin to think about how to tell her mother that she and Kyle were... What were they again? Dating? She didn't think she could call it that, exactly. But they'd agreed there was something between them and that they would take it slowly.

What exactly did *slowly* mean? Her palms grew slick when she pulled into the parking lot and saw Kyle's Denali parked next to Mark's vehicle. All these years she'd known Kyle and one simple kiss had flipped everything on its side, as if Nikki was the gondola in a balloon landing. Everything was jostled inside her now—both thrilling and terrifying.

How might he react to seeing her, or how did they act in front of Mark? She reminded herself that slow meant slow. She didn't intend to let him kiss her again until she was dead sure this would go in the right direction. She owed Michael that much.

After exiting her vehicle, she tromped through the puddles left from last night's rain and into the warehouse. She froze in the doorway.

Kyle and Mark were arguing, their raised voices carrying through the warehouse.

What in the world?

Although she hated to get in the middle, her curiosity wouldn't let her leave it alone. She forced her legs to move again and headed to Mark's office. Through the window, she saw his red face, and his eyes widened when he spotted her. But Kyle's back was to her, and he didn't know she was there. Didn't realize when she stood in the doorway.

"Why couldn't you have at least come to me first? Talk to me about it? Why do I have to hear it from someone else? I'm the one with experience. You have to talk her out of it."

"Talk me out of what," she said. But she knew exactly what had Kyle upset.

I should have told him.

Kyle stiffened, hesitating before he turned to face her. When he did, hurt flickered across his gaze, and his expression was torn, his face flushed with concern. Why would he get so upset over this?

"Why didn't you tell me?" he asked.

Nikki exhaled and moved to sit in the old rickety chair in the corner. That would give her time to formulate a response. "Because I wasn't sure how you would react."

"You didn't tell me because you knew exactly how I would react."

"Well, now you know, okay?" Nikki couldn't take his piercing glare and stared at Mark behind him. Who did Kyle think he was, anyway? Her protector? Then she remembered his promise to Jordan.

She remembered why Mark had talked to her alone. He'd wanted her decision, knowing, too, what Kyle's would be.

Kyle worked his jaw. Nikki had seen that plenty of times when he grew upset with Jordan. She'd never seen him direct that anger toward her, though.

"What about your piloting hours? Do you even have the hours for a gas balloon?"

What was he thinking? "They wouldn't let me in if I didn't."

He knew that. He also knew that Jordan had taught her everything she needed to know.

"You can't compete in a long race like that. Too much can go wrong," he said. "It's too dangerous."

Oh, that was it. Nikki knew she'd regret the words, but they had to be said. "If only you'd said those same words to Jordan."

Chapter 12

The next morning, Kyle stood in the warehouse, staring down at the slashed tires of a trailer. The trailer holding his balloon and parked inside their warehouse. Mark paced behind him.

Why hadn't the van tires been slashed instead? Parked outside, the two vans were easy to access.

In any case, Kyle had to reschedule his balloon flight. Couldn't exactly get the balloon outside and ready for passengers, chase the flight or bring it home without the trailer. Nor could he take Nikki's balloon because she had her own ride this morning. Besides, he was too upset. So he'd called Mark to come in during the early hours.

He had more than slashed tires on his mind.

After he'd learned Nikki's decision and Mark's part in it yesterday, he'd been stunned. Hadn't she told him about the job interview so he wouldn't be blindsided, as she'd put it? Then he'd gone off on her as though he had any right to tell her what she could do.

She'd been right to say those awful words before she'd walked out of the office on him. He'd let her go because her words had nailed him.

They rang in his ears.

Echoed in his heart.

Guilty as charged.

But why did the thought of her competing make him so crazy?

Especially when he and Jordan had always lived for thrills. Nikki, too, in her own way. Living life on the safe side had never been for any of them, but that came with a price. And he wasn't willing to pay or risk it where Nikki was concerned—part of his promise to Jordan.

He could still see the accident in his mind as if it had happened yesterday. Feel every whip of the wind on the gondola. The rapid descent of the balloon. Still see Jordan's face when he found his friend before the emergency crews could arrive. At the thought of Nikki competing in a similar long-distance race, pressure built around his heart.

God, how do I stop her?

And if he succeeded, she was so going to kill him for competing in the Gordon Bennett, after he'd been this adamant about her participation in a similar race. Watching her compete was one thing. Competing himself, another.

Besides, Nikki might have the necessary piloting hours, but she wasn't the kind of pilot for this type of race for a lot of reasons. One was the helium shortage. The balloons would be filled with hydrogen this year instead.

Highly flammable hydrogen.

Sure, hydrogen would take them the same distance—nothing would vary there. The difference lay in the way hydrogen reacted to changes in weather and temperature. Altitude and pressure. That meant more concentrated flying time around the clock. No sitting back for the ride.

It took a certain type of person. A certain breed of pilot.

A fearless person capable of enduring a grueling, risky flight.

Didn't she see that? If she didn't, Mark should—except he hadn't been around this sport long enough. And what about Michael? Was she even thinking about him? All these arguments he wished he could have made yesterday, but he knew she wouldn't listen.

And Kyle would never tell her that she wasn't a good enough pilot for the American Challenge competition unless he had to. He hoped it didn't come to that. He swiped a hand over his face and looked at the slashed tires again.

And now this. "Did you tell the police about the guy who used to work here that Nikki fired?"

"She told them, yes. I hope they questioned him, but I haven't heard anything." Mark squeezed Kyle's shoulder. "I'll call them again. File another report. This time we have the security camera."

"No, we don't," Kyle said. "Take a look outside. Someone must have climbed onto the roof to smash it so they wouldn't get caught while in the act."

"I'll check the video just the same."

"You do that, and let me know if it caught anyone before it was taken out. I have a few ideas of my own on how to catch this guy."

Kyle should have thought of this before, but he hadn't known the person bent on harassing them would go so far as to smash a security camera. That was gutsy. Next time he'd put a small video-recording device somewhere in the warehouse, and the guy wouldn't even know it. He could even monitor from his cell phone or computer at home. Maybe it was best to keep that secret from Mark, too. For all Kyle knew, Mark was involved, although the thought seemed as ridiculous as the vandalism that served no purpose.

Kyle sensed Mark's scrutiny.

"I can see those cogs in your mind grinding away," Mark said, "but just let the police handle this. I don't want to see anyone getting hurt."

"Slashed tires are one thing, but we have to do full inspections on these balloons on a weekly basis just to be safe. Nikki can't sell her business at a good price under these circumstances."

Not that he wanted her to. Kyle glanced at Mark to gauge his reaction. He hoped the guy didn't believe he had anything to do with this.

"I didn't think you were that keen on her selling out. And no, I don't think you're responsible for this. I can see that you care deeply about her." Mark crossed his arms and sighed. "I'm sorry I didn't include you in my conversation with Nikki about racing. It's her business. I wanted her opinion without your obvious influence."

My obvious influence? What did he mean by that?

"I get that," Kyle said. "I do. But what I don't get is why you'd want her to do it to begin with. How could you even ask her? And I don't get why she'd agree."

He sounded entirely too desperate, even to his own ears. Kyle hoped he could find another way to keep her out of it without having to hurt her or tarnishing her reputation as a pilot.

Mark moved in and crouched down to examine a tire. He fingered the slash. "You've been through a tragedy, son. You need to get your perspective back. This is a safe activity, for the most part. Accidents happen. But you get in your vehicle, steer it onto the road with hundreds of others and drive it every day without another thought."

Mark's comparison gave Kyle an idea.

"I might be a little nervous about that if someone had slashed my tires. Or cut the brake lines. We've called the police, installed a security system, and someone is still getting in here. Who is doing this? And don't tell me it's kids."

"I wish I had answers."

"What if someone wants to harm Nikki? Like you said, this is *her* business. This adds a new dynamic to her participation in the gas-balloon race, don't you think?"

Kyle hoped he was simply overreacting about the vandalism, considering everything he'd already been through. He hoped he was being overprotective of Nikki. That no one meant her harm.

When Mark peered up at him, doubt swam in his eyes. "I have no problem with you persuading her otherwise. You have more influence over her than I do. This was meant to help her efforts in selling the business, but I figured this would also go a long way in helping her to get over what happened to her brother. Even so, I'm not sure you'll be able to talk her out of competing."

Maybe he didn't have to. "Then I have something else in mind."

By the next Saturday, Nikki still wasn't talking to Kyle. Not really. She was distant.

Closed off.

He had the feeling the only reason she allowed him to take Michael fishing had everything to do with Michael's pleading and begging driving her nuts. So she'd let him go. She remained angry with Kyle for telling her she couldn't compete in the race—no doubt there. He wouldn't bother talking to her about his concerns until she was ready to listen.

But he and Mark were working on a new plan anyway.

He hoped his idea worked and she agreed. If only that would be enough to ease his own pain. To bury the wound she'd broken open with her words. The balloon accident was still between them. No point in pretending. But maybe this was all good, forcing them to face it.

Glancing in the rearview mirror, he could see Michael staring out the window. He wondered if the boy had ever been fishing. Kyle had planned for them to fish at Fenton Lake, but it was a little farther up the road, and Michael was eager to catch a fish. The Jemez River would serve his purpose just as well. Nikki's father used to take all three of them—Nikki, Jordan and Kyle—there to fish when they were kids. Everywhere he looked, the memories abounded.

He loved New Mexico and was glad he was back for the time being. Albuquerque was a truly breathtaking city. Coming in from the east, he'd had to drive over the Sandia Mountains. And there the city rested in all her splendor.

Clean and proud.

Heritage intact.

Indian and Mexican cultures evident everywhere.

He always loved the way the bridges and roads were painted with roadrunners and dream catchers—the old mixed in with the new. If he ended up staying, he'd want to build or purchase one of the gorgeous adobe houses. He'd always loved the architecture.

Kyle thought about Old Town and the Church Street Café with its twelve-inch-thick walls and the tile floors worn down from years of use. Maybe he'd take Nikki there on a date, if they ever actually had an official one.

With the rush of memories, he understood Nikki's reason for wanting to move away. And she was right—he'd had his chance to leave, to gain perspective.

Kyle sighed. The future seemed a little bleak.

"It looks like Mars," Michael said. "Do you think it looks like Mars?"

"The dirt is red, all right. Like something from a science-fiction movie, and the perfect place for us to stop and eat."

Despite her standoffish attitude, Nikki had sent them away with a couple of sandwiches and some drinks, giving her blessing. He wished she had come, too, but she claimed to be busy. He drove past a town of pueblo buildings and stopped at a small stand to buy some fry bread they could eat, too.

They found a picnic table, but eager to get to the reason for their trip, Michael ate only half his sandwich and barely touched the fry bread. "Can we go fishing now?"

Kyle chuckled and urged Michael to finish his sandwich first.

They found a place along the river, the Jemez Mountains a picturesque backdrop. Kyle finished securing a fish Michael had caught. Kyle's cell phone rang. He was surprised to get a signal out this way.

He glanced at the caller, and his heart thudded at the sight of Nikki's name. "Checking up on us already?"

She laughed. The pleasant and welcome sound sent relief through him. Her irritation with him must have lessened, at least a little. Now if he could get over his own hurt at her biting words.

"I wanted to let you know I have a balloon ride this evening. Would you mind keeping Michael a little longer? Mom…isn't feeling that well. I just…"

"I'll watch him. You know I will. We'll hang out for as long as you'll let us. We're buddies." He winked at Michael, knowing the boy was hanging on every word. She didn't need to explain to Kyle. When would she get it that he was there for her and Michael? When would any of them forget that he'd abandoned them, for all practical purposes? A close friend, he was like family, after all, and he'd just disappeared.

He hadn't forgiven himself on that point yet, either.

The line went silent long enough for him to wonder if he'd lost the connection. "You still there?"

"Yes." The way her voice cracked, he wondered if she'd been crying. "I'm sorry for what I said."

Now it was Kyle's turn to go silent. He needed to process her statement more. But how many years would he have to go through it with himself? With her? And she'd spoken the truth. He couldn't blame her for that.

He didn't have any idea how they could get past this to the relationship they both wanted. Nor was now the time to talk about any of it. Not in front of Michael.

So he changed the subject. "Hey, Michael caught a fish already."

"I hope you don't expect me to clean it." Nikki laughed, apparently willing to glide through her apology as well, though her voice sounded strained.

"Of course not. I've seen your attempt at cleaning fish," he said. And her definition of *filleting* was more like butchering.

She laughed, the sound making him wish he could crawl through the phone and be with her. Take her in his arms again. Forget the obstacles between them.

They said their goodbyes.

When he stuck the cell back in his pocket and got a better grip on his pole, Michael stared up at him, his forehead a little wrinkled. Too much worry for a boy so young. Kyle hated that he'd contributed to it.

"Don't worry, Uncle Kyle. She doesn't stay mad for long."

Perceptive boy, but Kyle wished the only problem between him and Nikki was her being mad at him.

"Thanks, little buddy."

"I think you need to call me Sheriff."

He was back to that again. Kyle laughed. "Sure thing, Sheriff."

* * *

Nikki didn't like to fly distracted.

With other people's lives in her hands, piloting a hot-air balloon required her attention, her concentration, despite there being so much out of her control. After all, a wicker basket held them all together suspended in the air, tied to a bag of hot air that drifted wherever the wind would take them.

Nikki's role as pilot was limited. The balloon would rise with more heat and sink when she vented the envelope. She had some control over where the wind took them by changing her vertical position up or down and catching a different wind direction at the right altitude.

So little control over the direction of her balloon, and really she was thinking more along the lines of her life, had never bothered her before. Flying was a tranquil experience, giving her and her clients a nature lover's high. Usually, the peace and quiet wrapped around her, calming her spirits even with clients present. It was the perfect quiet time with God—the silence so exceptional, it was impossible for others to understand. Her passengers often basked in the calmness, the serenity and the exquisite hushed escape from daily noise.

It was as if they suddenly became aware of their busy lives on the ground. And in the air, looking down on it all—the busyness seemed so remote and small. The clamor and din of life on earth was too much. How had they tolerated it for so long?

They enjoyed the view from the air and, if it weren't for that, might even forget they were in the air at all since the balloon moved along with the wind. The only time passengers could feel they were floating thousands of feet above the earth was during those periods when she would heat the envelope, causing it to rise or release air to descend into another current.

That was where Nikki was right now—her thoughts and heart, at least, were on the fact that her life was moving into another current. But was she ascending into a higher current, a current that would push her faster, or descending into a slower-moving current or dropping so fast that she would crash?

Her life had recently drifted along full of joy and peace. Why couldn't life stay the same? Why did it always have to change? Nikki shook the melancholy off. She had to land the balloon in the approaching field and began the slow descent, floating along at less than eight miles an hour.

She vented the balloon and then gave it a little more gas to even out the descent. Already she could see the chase car, David, Richard and Lenny waiting in the field, their designated landing point. They'd hold the basket down once she landed. Kyle's basket. Nikki'd had to use Kyle's balloon today, *Daydreamer*. The balloon belonged to Sky High, but Kyle had always used this one.

Mark had replaced the tires on the trailer, but now he wanted to inspect her balloon, *Wind Chaser,* again before she took it out. What was going on? Who was messing with them? Who cared enough about her little balloon business? Maybe Kyle was right to suggest Nathan was mad for getting fired. Whoever it was had taken out the security camera, so they hadn't been able to see a thing. The vandalism was only one of her worries, and it seemed to come out of nowhere—just tacked on to her already overburdened load.

The ground approached slowly, and Nikki instructed her passengers again—a warm and friendly couple and their little girl—about how to prepare for landing. She hated that she'd not given them her best today, but they probably enjoyed the ride regardless of her lack of input.

"Remember, this can be a little rough. We'll likely bump along the ground as the balloon gradually comes to a stop." The point was, she had to minimize any chance of a hard land. That was when people got hurt.

Jordan.

But 99 percent of the time, the passengers were exhilarated, feeling as if they'd just experienced one of life's high points, and they would be right.

Suddenly the wind picked up—a gust, ten, fifteen miles per hour. The basket bounced and dragged then hopped a few more times. The couple held on tightly and even laughed. The girl whimpered.

Then wind caught the envelope and dragged them for several yards before David and Richard were able to catch them and hold them down. Nikki had experienced a high-wind landing before.

Nothing to it.

Only this time, she was shaking a little. She started to climb from the basket when strong arms gripped her and pulled her out.

"Kyle?" *What is he doing here?* "And Michael?"

Kyle assisted the couple and their daughter and turned on all his charm to smooth over their experience in case they weren't happy. The man loved it, but his wife frowned at him, holding their child.

David escorted them over to his vehicle, where they were to wait while Richard and Lenny disassembled the envelope and basket so they could put it back in the trailer. Kyle pulled her aside. Michael was looking at the basket while Richard worked to completely deflate the balloon before the wind caused more problems.

Kyle's hands gripped her shoulders. "You okay?"

She nodded. "Of course. Why wouldn't I be?"

"That was a rough landing."

"Not at all." She shrugged him off and moved over to the basket to help the crew detach the balloon envelope.

"Oh, no." Nikki touched the uprights—the bars on the basket that held up the burner. "I think they're damaged."

"Let me see."

Nikki stepped back so Kyle could get closer. "I'm not sure we can even get this off the basket without some additional tools."

David and Richard looked on, both wearing frowns.

Kyle stood to his full height and peered down at Nikki, though he wasn't that much taller. "The bars look irreparable. I think we might have to order new ones. We'll take a closer look back at the warehouse."

Nikki read in his eyes what he wouldn't say. He was glad no one had been hurt.

"We pride ourselves on safety, you know," she said. Maybe she'd needed to reassure herself.

Kyle nodded and glanced at the clients. Nikki followed his gaze. Even the wife was smiling now. The husband was laughing. At least they'd enjoyed the ride. But she and Kyle felt the near-hard landing more keenly than the others ever would.

She wasn't sure what possessed her, but she took a step forward, and Kyle, seeming to read her mind, or at least want the same thing, wrapped his arms around her and held tight. She loved the feel of his arms around her—missed them, if she was honest with herself, though she'd experienced very little of his comforting embrace.

"Please don't fly in the American Challenge, Nikki," he whispered in her ear.

Nikki stiffened and stepped away from Kyle.

Chapter 13

Nikki looked out the window of the 747 and watched the jet's approach to Albuquerque—so different from watching the city while floating above in a hot-air balloon.

The same in many ways, yet different. The jet was faster, bumpier, and the whine of the engine grated at the back of her neck. Definitely not the peaceful experience of ballooning.

The fiesta was only a week away, and already the city was beginning to look busier than usual, or was Nikki simply imagining it because her life was far too busy?

Next week, the traffic would be unbearable.

Next week, Nikki would be flying in a gas balloon on the race of her life. She was actually more of a token pilot on an already-experienced team that had been practicing for the competition; she knew that—kudos to Mark.

But they would be in the air for days. What had she been thinking to agree? Kyle's insistence that she not compete had only solidified her decision.

Decisions made for those kinds of reasons were never good decisions. She knew that. And yet, she couldn't bring herself to back down. It didn't help that her mother had been hurt and angry when she'd told her the news.

The jet hit turbulence, and Nikki gripped the armrests, grateful no one sat next to her. Once the flight smoothed out a little, she rubbed her eyes. Adding to everything, she'd had an interview in Tulsa.

Things were moving along far too fast for her. She thought she'd send out her résumé and it would take months, maybe even a year, before she received any interest. Finding a job outside of where you lived was toughest of all.

She'd watched that happen to friends and others around her plenty of times. But the old adage that said it was not about what you knew, but *who* you knew had definitely come into play here. It had even come into play regarding the upcoming balloon competition.

The jet appeared to circle Albuquerque for another try at landing. Nikki couldn't wait to be on the ground again. She missed Michael and her mother.

And…she missed Kyle in a powerful way. Why did she need him so much?

To distract her from the anxiety, she shut her eyes and recalled her conversation with Jeff, the man who'd interviewed her for the job with Cyntrex Energy. He was serious about hiring her because she'd come highly recommended by his sister. Nikki had done work for Tina for a few years now, and they'd become friends. Talk about putting the pressure on. Tina would absolutely kill her if she messed this up.

She cringed inside to think that she'd gone this far with the process, allowing them to fly her out there for an interview. If she didn't go forward, she'd feel as if she'd let a friend and client down. Although she didn't owe Tina or Tina's brother anything, Nikki didn't want to take advantage of anyone's generosity.

To his credit, Jeff had given her time to decide. He appeared to understand what she'd be giving up—the only life she'd ever known. And yet, he'd taken her need to escape seriously and was willing to give her a chance to start fresh.

What kind of person would do that?

Kyle's face came into her thoughts. Deep down, she knew she hadn't given him that fresh start he'd wanted with his return. But how did a person do that? How did she truly let go of lingering resentment and bitterness? She thought she had, but when she'd been pushed, everything inside had erupted again. She could hardly forgive herself, much less Kyle.

How did she forgive and *forget*?

Nikki recognized the impossible. She reminded herself that all things were possible with God. There was that, yes. But didn't it require her participation on some level? She wasn't sure.

The jet bumped the runway, hopped a couple of times and then found traction. Nikki chuckled to herself. She was there—bumping along, still looking for that grip on her life. She'd told Jeff to give her until after the fiesta, and she'd let him know her answer. Then she'd give him her commitment to moving what was left of her family to Tulsa for a fresh start. Or not.

She'd never known anything but Albuquerque and balloons. Was leaving the right decision?

Nikki waited in her seat as others claimed their carry-on items from the overhead bins. Then there was Kyle—she still wasn't sure if there could ever be anything between them—but the problem was, she already had strong feelings for him because she'd harbored those feelings much of her life.

Oh, Lord, why?

When it was her turn to go, she waited and allowed a threesome family—a man, woman and their young child—to go before her. Much of Sky High's business centered around romance, so why did Nikki struggle with it so much on a personal level?

While she stood in the aisle and slowly followed the other passengers out, she turned her thoughts to Michael and Mom, who insisted on picking her up at the airport when Nikki could easily have driven herself. Michael would be out of school by now, too. Maybe they could grab supper on the way home.

She suspected Mom was trying to show support for whatever move Nikki decided on. It wasn't like Mom had to go with her. She was a grown woman who could remain in New Mexico. But they agreed for Michael they would keep their simple family intact.

Did that simple family already include Kyle? She suspected if she were to ask Michael, he would say it did. She didn't know if she'd made a mistake or not in allowing Michael to spend so much time with Kyle, but the boy needed a man in his life, a father figure. And Kyle had filled the title like a real hero come to their rescue. She could almost forget that he'd disappeared for three years.

Almost.

She'd yet to truly understand why. Maybe she did understand, but understanding or not, she couldn't imagine being in his shoes and leaving like that.

A mesh of confusion clouding her thoughts, Nikki sighed and stepped from the plane onto the Jetway that connected the plane to the terminal. Turning her mind to thoughts of Michael, she allowed herself to be herded along until she stepped into the airport terminal, her gaze searching for her small family.

And there, at the front of the few people gathered to meet disembarking family or friends, stood Kyle, holding a bouquet of flowers—daffodils, white chrysanthemums and purple hyacinths.

Beautiful.

Nikki froze, and someone bumped into her from behind. Her breath caught in her throat. Tears burned her eyes.

Kyle brought me flowers?

His dimpled smile that she'd always loved—no doubt there—sent a quiver through her knees. Not now. She had to be strong.

Michael peeked from behind him. "Hi, Mommy."

He'd called her Mommy?

Nikki found enough traction for the moment to move forward and out of the stream of passengers that moved around her. She set her briefcase on the floor and hugged Michael to her, overwhelmed by it all.

When Michael escaped her grip, Kyle handed her the flowers.

"These are for you," he said, his grin a little nervous and hesitant.

Cute.

"Thank you." Nikki took them and smelled their sweetness, touched by his old-fashioned thoughtfulness.

"I'm sorry," he said, the grin finally faltering completely.

For everything. "For trying to tell you what to do."

Kyle worked to keep his face, his smile, steady. He didn't realize how much he would miss her when she left, how much her going to interview in person for the job would affect him. But he shoved that aside to deal with what he could control.

Regret had accosted him, and he felt it to his core, but he had to convince Nikki he meant the apology because he needed to persuade her to go along with the plan he and Mark had devised while she was away. And that after he delivered some not-so-good news.

Too bad she might see his apology as a way of manipulating her, softening her up, even though he truly was sorry. He ignored the guilt clawing at him—he hated everything that seemed to stand in the way of what he wanted with Nikki.

Beautiful Nikki.

She studied him, her eyes searching for the truth in his words, and he shoved aside the realization that her hesitation to accept his apology stung a little.

"These are lovely. You pick them out yourself?"

Encouraged, he forced his wavering smile to reach his eyes. "I had a little help, yes. The flowers are supposed to symbolize an apology."

"I see." The gleam in her eyes said she was toying with him.

He thrust his hand out, hiding his inward cringe at his own clumsy way with her. "Friends?"

A soft smile played at the corners of her mouth as she dipped her face to the flowers once again, a bashful flutter to her lashes as she closed her eyes and drew in a breath.

He stifled the chuckle welling inside. She was making him wait for it. And wait for it he would. Forever, if he had to. The thought startled him. Finally, she opened her lids, and her wide-eyed, transparent gaze took him aback as she placed her small hand in his.

"Friends," she said, her voice soft. Feminine.

Kyle held her hand as they made their way to the baggage claim. He didn't want to let go. She'd stayed over only one night, during which she'd had dinner with her potential future boss.

The three of them strolled through the airport corridor, hand in hand, like a real family.

"Told you Mommy wouldn't stay mad for long."

Mommy.

Kyle glanced over Michael's head at Nikki and winked. Did she feel the rush of love at hearing Michael call her that? Or a rush of unbidden memories of when Michael's mother had left? Or Jordan's death?

God, will we ever get over this?

At the baggage claim, Kyle urged Nikki to stand back with Michael while he grabbed her bag from the baggage carousel. He needed time to gather his thoughts again. Figure out how he would tell her the bad news. And then what he needed to say to ease into their new plans for the fiesta.

He almost wished Mark was here with him to help convince her, and in the end, it might come to that. But Mark had assured him that Kyle held more sway over Nikki.

Kyle lifted the bag from the carousel, scoffing to himself. Yeah, right. It was because of his so-called sway that she'd been more than determined to continue with what everyone seemed to understand was a bad call—the American Challenge. That wasn't something Nikki could or should do at this moment in time, even if she was only a so-called token pilot.

Nikki tried to wrestle her bag from him, but he held strong. "I've got it. You hold Michael's hand while I get the Denali."

"You seem a little tense. Everything all right?"

"Of course."

Kyle knew he should ask her about how the interview had gone, but that was a tough one. *After I get the Denali.*

He found a bench where they could wait. "We can walk with you, Kyle," she said. "The parking garage isn't that far."

The way she said the words, soft and compelling, Kyle wondered which of them was the more persuasive one. "Okay, have it your way."

She laughed, and he treasured the easy conversation. He hadn't been sure how she would receive him when he arrived instead of her mother. "I contacted your mother about picking you up, just so you know. Turns out she had a headache and wasn't feeling like navigating through traffic."

"I told her that she wouldn't want to pick me up. I don't know what she was thinking by insisting."

Kyle knew what she was thinking. For once, Nikki's mother and Kyle were a team. Neither of them wanted to see Nikki race the American Challenge. Not with Michael watching, knowing what had happened to his father, though it was a different gas-balloon race.

In the vehicle, he steered from the parking lot and out of the airport. Michael chattered away in the backseat about how well school had gone since the bully issue had subsided.

Nikki's pleasure at the news was almost palpable, but she kept glancing at Kyle. He was never good at hiding anything from her. She knew he had an agenda. He looked in the mirror and switched lanes, acting as if all his focus was on driving.

"So, how did the job interview go?" Let her think his anxiety was over the possibility of her leaving, and that would be partly, if not mostly, true.

She'd be walking out on them before they even had a chance. Kyle couldn't exactly follow her there without some sort of permanency to their relationship—and right now, it looked as if they needed distance and perspective.

I'm running out of time. By the set of her jaw at his question, he could see that he might even drive her away, if he wasn't careful.

"Fine. It was good." She eyed him, gesturing to the backseat, letting him know she didn't feel comfortable discussing the subject in front of Michael. Was that the only reason?

Would she tear Michael away from Kyle?

The manner in which he'd picked her up at the airport was meant to establish a truce and, in a sense, allow them to start over. Again. But it wasn't working. There was too much tension for him to break the news to her. But if not now, then when?

"Listen, we had a problem while you were gone."

She shifted in her seat. "What?"

"Everything's okay, but someone stole one of the trailers." Kyle hated breaking the news to her like this. He wanted to watch her expression. He steered into the parking lot of a steak house. "Who's hungry?"

"I am." Michael bounced in the backseat, despite his restraints.

Nikki glared at him.

Kyle Morgan, you are an idiot.

"Just tell me what happened. You don't have to soften me up."

"I'm not trying to soften you up. I'm hungry. I had planned to take you to eat."

She pursed her lips, and he figured she was thinking that he'd made the decision without bothering to ask her. He was racking up the negative points and fast.

"I had planned to ask you if you'd like to go eat." He flashed a grin, hoping he could salvage his quickly deflating balloon.

Michael had unbuckled and leaned over the front seat. "Don't you love the flowers Uncle Kyle bought you?"

A smile tugged at the corners of her mouth. "You two are in cahoots. I can tell."

Kyle held his palms up in mock innocence.

She shook her head, seeming to internalize what he'd just told her about the trailer. "Sure, why not. And you'd better tell me *everything* that happened, Kyle Morgan."

Kyle smiled, loving it when she called him by his full name, even though that was always meant to be part of a threat when they were growing up. He stepped from the vehicle, but she didn't wait for him to open the door for her and met him halfway in front of the grille.

Michael was still climbing out.

"Tell me what else, Kyle. Right now. A trailer and what else?"

"Yes, they took your balloon, which was inside." *This isn't how I wanted to tell her...*

She cupped her hands over her face and sniffled.

Kyle stepped closer and wrapped her in his arms, unsure if she'd refuse his comfort as she'd done only a few nights ago after the hard landing. "It's going to be all right. The police are working on it. It's not like a person can easily hide a trailer like that or the balloon. It's not like we wouldn't see it floating in the sky." *Crazy.*

"I don't understand. Why would someone do that? Why is all this happening just when I'm trying to sell the business?"

"We'll figure this out," he said, offering reassurance, though he wasn't at all impressed with the investigation.

Michael came up behind her and got in on the hugs.

Kyle released her. "Come on. Let's get something to eat."

He'd give her time to digest what had happened before he brought up the rest.

Chapter 14

After dinner, Kyle took her and Michael home.

They'd shared small talk through the meal because Michael was there. Nikki hoped for a chance to talk to Kyle alone to find out what else was bothering him. As if there needed to be anything else. But she could tell something more was on his mind.

Probably her interview.

Back at the house, Nikki put the beautiful and thoughtful flowers in a vase while Kyle played video games with Michael until his bedtime. Her mother appeared to be over the headache that had kept her from driving to the airport.

Leaning against the doorjamb, she watched Kyle and Michael playing while she sipped a cup of tea and her mother made a blueberry pie. She needed to call Tina to tell her about the interview with Tina's brother, but Nikki wasn't certain how she felt about any of it. Not about the job or the move. Not about the vandalism and theft at Sky High.

Not about Kyle and her.

Not about Kyle and her nephew.

And yet warmth flooded her insides as she watched the two of them so intent, smiling and enjoying themselves. Bonding.

"It's time for bed, Michael. And don't you have an early flight in the morning, Kyle?" They didn't react as if they'd heard her, so engrossed were they in the game. Nikki wasn't in the frame of mind to press them at the moment.

What were they going to do with just one working balloon? With Jordan's old balloon still waiting to be repaired and her *Wind Chaser* stolen, this could devastate the business. Neither Kyle nor Chase had any reason to stay on if they couldn't fly. How would she ever sell the business now unless they recovered the balloon? Mark had already filed a claim with the insurance company, Kyle had assured her.

Before she realized it, he stood directly in front of her and took the cup from her hands. Her mother ushered Michael out of the room and to bed. What was going on? Everyone was working together behind her back, it seemed.

"Let's go for a walk," Kyle said.

She gazed into his smoky blues. Did he want to walk with her because he simply wanted to spend time with her? She wished that was the only reason. But no. It was obvious he had more to discuss. They both did.

They walked in silence, holding hands again the way they had at the airport, making their way around the block and to a small neighborhood park. Nikki wished she could forget all the events and confusion swirling inside and just enjoy Kyle. Be with him as she'd imagined so many times when she was younger. But she was a grown woman now—and nothing in life was simple.

Kyle pressed his hand against the small of her back, ushering her to a park bench. A small thing, really, but the touch of his hand, his gentleness, turned her insides to mush.

"Let's sit here while we talk."

"I'm not sure I want to hear this. I've had a long day already." Too much bad news. Too many decisions.

"I told you I was sorry today. Do you believe me?"

"You mean, do I think it was all part of some sort of ploy so that it would be easier to tell me the news about the stolen balloon and trailer?"

Kyle chuckled and gazed up at the stars. When he looked back at her, he said, "I meant the words, Nikki. I'm sorry for so much. But there's something else, and I need you to hear me out."

Nikki leaned against the bench, feeling pressed with the weight of dread. "Go on."

"I was wrong to tell you that you shouldn't compete in the gas-balloon race. I know that. Mark and I came up with a plan that we think will work better to benefit the business. Better than your having to leave Michael and your mother to fly across the country for days in a gas balloon."

Nikki stiffened and opened her mouth—

Kyle lifted a hand to stop her. "It's your decision. Just hear me out."

Nikki sighed. More than anything, she wanted to get to her feet and walk away. But everything had drained her. "I'm listening."

"Mark and I, and your mother, I should add, have been concerned about the vandalism. We don't know if someone is targeting you or just the business or what. I guess you could say that adds fuel to the fire of anxiety about your competing in the more complicated, more grueling and lengthy race."

"And?"

"We thought it might be more prudent to enter the more

localized competitions that take place at the fiesta. There would be much more publicity for Sky High that way. You and I could fly together, compete together."

"All the planning you two, or you three, have been doing behind my back sounds wonderful." She made sure he didn't miss her sarcasm. "But you're forgetting one thing. It's too late. I barely got into the American Challenge as it is, and that thanks to Mark's networking savvy. Sky High hasn't participated in the actual fiesta in three years. We're just way busier during the fiesta with balloon rides. But now we can't even do that because someone has stolen one of our three balloons and we're still waiting on repairs on the other one."

Her voice grew shaky with the tears that twisted in her throat.

"That can all be arranged, Nikki. We have a sponsored balloon waiting for us to fly if you choose to do this. There is someone ready to step in and take your place in the American Challenge. An alternate, if you will."

Connections meant everything. Nikki knew that to be true, even with the interview in Tulsa. "You guys have put a lot of thought into this, haven't you?"

Could they be that worried about her?

"I think this will do more for Sky High, in the end." Kyle scooted closer to her and took her hand in his.

"And this is my decision?" she asked.

He nodded. "Of course."

"Look me in the eyes and tell me you haven't already made the arrangements."

He hesitated and then said, "I can't."

Nikki found the energy to stand. "How could you do that without my permission? How dare you do that?"

She stomped away and headed home, Kyle on her heels. "Stop following me. I need to be alone."

He pushed past and stood in her path.

"Get out of my way."

He took her hand and held on, gently. "Nikki," he whispered.

Hearing the sound of her name on his lips that way, she stumbled a little then stopped. "I just need time to think about it."

"Of course you do," he said, but he was sincere. Not patronizing.

"It's like everything is spinning out of my control."

He drew near, lifting her face to look her in the eyes. "Give me some credit. I tried to be gentle, to let you make the decision, and it's still yours to make. But I want to keep my promise to your brother, too."

Nikki wanted to throw that back in his face, but he was right. He was trying to honor his promise to Jordan.

"Is that all I am to you?" Oh, why had she blurted that out?

Kyle inched closer, his face near hers now.

Nikki debated stepping back, but the longing to be near Kyle encapsulated her, holding her in place.

"You should know by now that, regardless of my promise to Jordan, I care deeply for you." His breath fanned her lips before his mouth connected with hers, connecting with her heart. Nikki slipped her arms around Kyle's neck, savoring the tenderness in his kiss. Savoring that he made her feel cherished. When he drew back, he pressed his nose against hers and sighed with contentment.

Nikki could almost feel as if this was always meant to be. Why had it taken them so long? Jordan should never have stood in their way.

"Is this supposed to be part of your persuasion technique?" she asked.

His grin was mischievous. "No, but is it working?"

Nikki both loved and hated how he made her feel. She sighed in reply.

"When do you need an answer?" she asked. "I assume you needed to know yesterday."

"A week ago, actually, but we waited until you got back from your interview."

They'd been planning this that long? Talking behind her back? Nikki tried to pull away at the revelation, but Kyle pinned her against him and teased her lips with his again. "I can't think of anything I'd rather do than spend the fiesta with you floating above the earth in a balloon, Nikki Alexander."

"I see why Mark sent you to do the dirty work. I think you just sealed the deal," she said. "But you had an unfair advantage."

While she was in his arms, the job in Tulsa, selling the business and even the theft and vandalism seemed to take place in a distant country. She was such a pushover when it came to this man.

Tomorrow she would wake up and all the issues would weigh heavy on her again. She couldn't even be sure that Kyle would still be there. She'd been through that before.

He hadn't asked her for more details about her interview, but she understood why. Their relationship could only handle so much at one time.

Later that evening, Kyle stood on the balcony of his apartment and leaned over the railing, a cool breeze licking at his face as if joining in his big sigh of relief. A sigh that left him breathless.

Nikki had agreed to everything.

But not without making him work for it. He smiled to himself, remembering their kiss. It had been worth it. Oh, so worth it.

Elbows pressed on the railing, he rested his chin in his hand. Next week this city would be crazy with balloon enthusiasts from all over the country, and in fact, the world. Kyle would participate in the competitions with Nikki, who had quickly turned into his dream girl—that was, if she didn't plan to leave him behind when and if she moved.

He still had something else to tell her—his last promise to Jordan—and he knew Nikki well enough. She was not going to like it.

Why hadn't he told her that first night when he'd shared with her that Jordan had made him promise to watch out for her and Michael? Then he wouldn't have to worry about severing their relationship when it was so fragile. But he knew why. He'd been too afraid that she wouldn't even allow him to stay. Telling her had been too risky then and was still too risky now.

He'd hoped they would be further along by now, because it wasn't as if he could put off telling her much longer. She would find out on her own soon enough. Kyle had to be the one to tell her, but finding the right time hadn't exactly been easy.

Someone knocked on his door. He glanced at his watch—nine-thirty?—and made his way through the sliding glass door and across the living room. Who would stop by this late?

Kyle opened the door to see Mark standing there with a concerned expression. "I tried to call. You weren't answering."

Kyle opened the door wide to let the man in. He remembered then that his phone rested on the table with the ringer off. He hadn't wanted any interruptions while he was with Nikki. "Sorry, I didn't hear the phone."

"Did she accept?"

"I should have called you. I just got home and was

thinking through everything." Kyle swiped a hand through his hair. "And yes," he added quickly. "We're good to go."

Mark sagged with relief that rivaled Kyle's own. "Did you tell her we'd already made the arrangements?"

"She knows." Kyle plopped onto the sofa and gestured for Mark to sit, too.

He obliged. "How did she take it?"

"When I left her she was fine." Sort of. "Tomorrow might be different, but I think she has too much going on to throw much of a fit."

"I didn't trust you at first, Kyle, but you did well. This is the right thing for everyone."

Though Kyle grated at Mark's admission of distrust, that he respected him now made him feel better. Mark was a good man. Except there was something else, something bordering on an accusation behind his eyes.

"Did she tell you anything about the job interview?" Mark stood and edged toward the door as if he'd never planned to stay long.

"Not much." Kyle frowned and stared through the sliding glass door he'd left open. They hadn't gotten to that with everything else.

"I have some news about the stolen balloon and trailer. The police looked at the video you captured, and even though the guy wore a mask, the police are looking for Nathan to question him. He disappeared. If he's our guy, then maybe he's on the run. With or without our balloon and trailer, I don't know. But if we can get this behind us and retrieve the balloon, that will go a long way toward getting the business sold. I've had a couple of inquiries, but nothing serious yet."

Kyle stood, too, and jammed his hands in his pockets, suddenly feeling worn out from his efforts today. He wished his hidden webcam surveillance he'd set up in the warehouse had done more. "I hope they get the guy. But I'll be honest—I hate to see Nikki sell her business. I think she'll regret it later."

Mark studied Kyle's russet-colored carpet. "I know you care about her, but you have to consider what's best for her and the boy. That brings me to the other reason I stopped by."

When Mark's gaze snapped back to Kyle, his eyes narrowed. "I heard something today, so I thought I'd ask you about it. Didn't even do any research before I came over. I wanted to hear this from you. After you were so adamant that Nikki not compete in the long-distance race, and the trouble we've gone through to get her out of it, I couldn't believe my ears…" Mark let his words trail off, already seeing in Kyle's eyes the truth.

Add to that, the pain Nikki and her family had gone through and the role Kyle had played in it. Kyle's throat suddenly felt as if it had been cinched off by a cord, restricting his air. He looked away. If he could have found his voice, he couldn't have found the words.

When Kyle didn't say anything, his silence confirmation enough, Mark continued, "Did you tell her?"

"Not yet."

"When were you going to tell *me?*"

"Um…"

Though Kyle was glad they still had Chase to pilot if they ever got more than one balloon offering rides again, Kyle would be unavailable for a while. The balloon fiesta started Friday of *next* week, and the Gordon Bennett two weeks after that. Kyle was already mentally gearing up. He'd need to start training with the other member of his team soon, which meant some of his flying time would be taken from what he did with Sky High. The Gordon Bennett started in France this year, so he'd be gone that week.

What a jerk he was.

Chapter 15

Hundreds of balloons of all sizes and shapes grew from crumpled, vibrantly colored sheets on the ground like painted hills rising from the earth as crews worked to get their balloons inflated. Once they were ready, they remained tethered to the ground, awaiting the final countdown until the balloon-glow event.

The anticipation in Fiesta Park was palpable.

The morning mass ascension had been canceled along with the races that day. Strong winds had a way of disrupting the world's largest balloon event, but balloon enthusiasts weren't deterred and were out in the thousands.

Hundreds of thousands, even.

Tonight, officials had given the go-ahead, and Nikki was ready to go.

The sponsored balloon that she and Kyle had agreed to pilot, though colorful, could hardly keep Michael's attention like the neighboring balloons—the blue-faced Smurf, hippopotamus, soccer ball and SpongeBob himself—all closed in around them as they grew to their full size.

Michael pointed out the bumblebees on the far side—they were among the favorites every year. Along with other popular and easily recognizable characters, stood Darth Vader and Yoda, silhouetted against the setting sun.

Soccer balls, sodas and cartoon-animal faces. Nikki delighted in Michael's wide-eyed giggles over the monkey balloon. She squeezed her nephew, who now called her the most treasured endearment in the world.

Mommy.

It had started slow at first.

When he'd first called her that at the airport, Nikki hadn't had it in her heart to correct him. She wasn't Michael's mother, nor had she expected to replace his mother, and she wasn't even sure he should call her Mommy. But somehow it felt right—she was the only mother he'd known since he was very young.

She glanced past Michael at Kyle, who stayed in the gondola, his hand gripping the propane-release valve. He smiled at her, eyes overflowing with an emotion she'd only dreamed she'd ever see there. Could she be imagining that look in his eyes?

"Thank you," she whispered, knowing he couldn't hear the words above the pop music that echoed around them, mingling with hundreds of voices. But she knew he'd read the words on her lips, just the same.

His dimpled grin spread wider with his quiet reply. "You're welcome."

They had an understanding—the two of them. He had to know exactly why she'd thanked him. If it wasn't for his determination in redirecting her competition participation during the fiesta, she'd have missed this moment. If it wasn't for Kyle and Mark, she'd be with her gas-balloon team, inflating their balloon, which would take off shortly after the balloon glow. She would have been gone for two or three days. Relief swept across her heart.

If she glanced across the way to the gas-balloon launch site, she might catch a glimpse of the more spherical envelopes of the gas balloons preparing to launch tonight.

"Look, Mommy," Michael said.

A thrill rushed through Nikki again when he called her that. "What is it?"

"A shark. You see the shark?"

The sky was growing darker with each moment, and the field grew more crowded as the balloons became fully inflated. She searched between the hundreds of shapes and spotted the shark Michael referred to.

The excited crowd, hundreds of colorful balloons, the music, along with her favorite people in the world—Kyle and Michael, the Sky High crew, and even her mother stood in the midst of the Albuquerque International Balloon Fiesta.... Nikki hadn't felt this elated in years.

This was almost like old times.

Once all the balloons were inflated, though still anchored to the ground, the crowd joined in singing the national anthem, and then the countdown began.

"Michael, you hear that? Let's count," she said. "Five, four, three, two, one."

And then Kyle and all the other pilots fired their propane burners.

Fiesta Park lit up with the glow of scores of balloons.

Awe-filled laughter seemed to harmonize with the music. Nikki lifted Michael in her arms and squeezed him, swinging him around, allowing her heart to soar with the moment.

"You look like you're having way more fun than me,"

Kyle said. "Why don't you come help me light the balloon up, Sheriff Michael?"

Michael quickly scrambled from her arms and made his way to the basket. David helped him climb inside with Kyle, who tossed Nikki a triumphant, teasing grin.

"Oh, no, you don't." Nikki wasn't about to let him have all the fun. "It's my turn to light things up."

She hefted herself on the side of the basket, the sponsor's basket much smaller than the commercial size that Sky High used. Kyle grabbed her waist and assisted her inside, and though she didn't need his help—having done this thousands of times in her life—she liked the way he made her feel. For a moment, he held her close, his hands on her waist, protective, reassuring, as he stared down at her.

And the basket was so small. No place to escape. She almost regretted the move. Kyle was so. Very. Close.

The balloon glow faded into a distant backdrop, yet became the perfect ambience—hundreds of candles dancing on the night air. Nikki longed for him to kiss her, but she didn't want an audience. She sensed that he was hesitant to break their connection, too, but Michael was there with them, waiting. She had a feeling even some of their crew watched from the sidelines. Surely she and Kyle weren't more interesting than the balloon glow.

The look Kyle gave her warmed her heart even as he took a step back. "She's yours when you want her."

Wrapping her hand around the lever, Nikki never wanted to leave the warm cocoon Kyle had wrapped her in. Releasing the propane, the resulting flame lit up the faces of the small family in the basket.

"I want to do it." Michael tugged on her arm.

Nikki shook her head. Hadn't she meant to protect Michael from this world that had killed his father? She wasn't sure when it had happened, but at some point she'd started believing she'd been wrong to ever think about moving Michael away from his heritage.

The accident was just that. An accident.

She had already accepted that there wasn't anyone to blame anymore, if there ever was. Then why couldn't Nikki completely let go?

Kyle shifted in the basket. "I've got this."

Nikki stepped aside so Kyle could lift Michael into his arms. "Put your hand against mine," he said.

Michael pressed his small hand over Kyle's as he gripped the lever. The flame roared to life, heating the air inside the envelope.

Michael had been so young when Jordan died, he didn't remember much about his father. Kyle was a natural with Michael, quickly stepping in and taking Jordan's place as though it was always meant to be that way. A strange mix of sadness and joy twisted in her heart.

"That's it, Sheriff Michael," Kyle said, his voice oddly laced with emotion. "You're getting the hang of it."

Just like your father.

When Kyle turned to look at her, she could almost believe he'd read her mind just then.

Michael's hand pressed over his, the boy squeezed as if he believed he had contributed to lighting the balloon.

Kyle knew that a deep love for balloons was ignited in Michael's heart at that moment. Overwhelming joy, a sense of contentment, swam in his own heart. Michael laughing like the happiest boy in the world, and Nikki watching the two of them, love in her eyes. Of course, the emotion emanating from her had everything to do with Michael, but Kyle had a feeling that she felt the same for him, and it was more than just the attraction they shared or their love for each other as lifelong friends.

"Mommy, look. Look! I'm doing it, too. I can fly balloons, too!"

"I see that," she said, her smile for Michael, but her eyes on Kyle.

Was she angry or upset? Worried that Michael would follow in his father's footsteps?

"Don't you think I'll make a good pilot?" he asked, but his question was directed at Kyle this time.

Kyle searched Nikki's gaze, watching her reaction. He didn't want to urge Michael in a direction Nikki didn't want him to go, but he couldn't read her. She seemed strangely resigned to things, and that didn't seem like her at all.

"I think you'll be great at whatever you set your mind on." Kyle grinned. Who could argue with that?

As the balloon-glow event died down, Kyle was well aware that the gas balloons across the way were preparing to make their launch for the adventure of a lifetime—flying across the country over two or three days or even longer. But as he enjoyed this time with Nikki and Michael, he felt as if he was on the adventure of a lifetime already. By the look of things, it didn't appear Nikki regretted pulling out of the American Challenge.

After they assisted the crew in deflating and packing the balloon in the trailer, Kyle, Nikki, Michael, Nikki's mother and Mark headed over to watch the fireworks. The days ahead would be one of the longest weeks of his life with the early-morning Dawn Patrols, competitions and other events that continued well after midnight. Chase would offer balloon rides from the Sky High field in their one and only balloon—*Daydreamer.* So things had worked out the way they should on that front, at least for the moment.

Michael was in school during the week of the fiesta, but Nikki's mother planned to bring him over to the park as soon as she could each day. As they strolled to the field where they could watch the fireworks, Kyle wondered if Nikki noticed the smile Mark seemed to put on her mother's face. After Jordan's death, her mother had struggled to let it go and look to the future, as they all had, but that had put a much greater burden on Nikki.

She sighed, taking in the sights and sounds, her gaze drifting to Mark and her mother, smiling at each other, sharing conversation. She didn't have a clue that Kyle was watching her, just as she watched them.

The fireworks lit up the sky, booming and popping. Nikki's mother held Michael's hand as they watched the show. Kyle remembered back to the moment when he'd assisted Nikki into the basket with him and Michael, and he slipped his hand around her small waist. He was fortunate to hear her quiet intake of breath when she glanced up at him.

Fortunate to see the soft smile slip onto her lips. He caught her waist again and swept her behind the concession stand, leaving the others to watch the fireworks without them. She giggled, putting up a feeble protest.

"Kyle," she said. "What are you doing? Everyone will wonder where we've gone."

"I don't care. I can't wait anymore."

"What are you talking about?"

Kyle leaned in and covered her mouth with his own, and feeling Nikki's resistance melt away, he wrapped his arms around her and drew her soft form against him. Her lips were soft and tender and tasted like strawberries. Must be the lip gloss. Breathless, Kyle ended the moment, drawing his face back but not too far. "I've wanted to do that all night."

She closed her eyes and smiled. Kyle was sure his own

contentment was reflected in her beautiful face. "Nikki."
His voice cracked a little. "Don't leave."

"I don't…I don't know, Kyle." Confusion coiled around
her words. "I have that job offer. I have to let him know
soon. This could be our chance."

"What about us?" Kyle asked. "What about *our* chance?"

He didn't want to pressure her, but what else could he
do? If she was really bent on leaving, then he could go with
her, but first, she needed to know everything. He needed
her to want him by her side, but on that he wouldn't pressure her.

Sensing her change in mood, that she was moments
from edging away, he tugged her closer and held her hand
pressed against his heart.

"I love you," he said.

There, everything was laid out for her. Well, not everything, but now wasn't the time to tell her *that* everything, though he was running out of time. But right now,
he wanted to hear her response to his declaration of love.

She exhaled, her warm breath fanning his face. "I love
you, too."

Kyle tried to kiss her, but Nikki forced some distance
from him this time. "I love you, too. I do."

The way she said those last two words warned Kyle
that she had something more to say and he wasn't going
to like it.

"But I have to think about Michael. I mean, he's calling
me Mommy. *Mommy.* I can't let anything or anyone stand
in the way of making the right decision for him."

Didn't Nikki see that they could be a family together?
Kyle could be the father that Michael had lost. Or was it
that she did see it, and that was not what she wanted?

He stepped back, swiping a hand through his hair. The
last thing Kyle wanted to do was pressure her. He might

have already done too much pressuring tonight. If he wasn't careful, she might kick him out of her life for good.

"You're right," he said. "Michael comes first."

He was surprised when she moved closer and slid her hands up his shoulders. "You already know that I love you. Just give me some time to figure things out. Let's enjoy ourselves through the fiesta. We have a race tomorrow, remember?"

"And the next day and the next day…" He trailed off, grinning.

She stood on her toes and pressed her lips against his. Kyle lowered his head to conform to her shorter height. For the next few days, he wouldn't worry about their future. He'd do as she suggested—enjoy what they had together for the moment.

I'm running out of time.

Chapter 16

Nikki climbed into the small gondola of the soft drink–sponsored red-and-white balloon she and Kyle would fly in today's competitions.

The familiar click of a camera behind her caught her attention. A lively smile slipped naturally onto her face, and she nudged Kyle. He turned around and wrapped his arm around Nikki's shoulders, drawing their faces close for the photograph. Nikki wasn't certain she was ready to see a picture she was sure portrayed them as a couple slapped all over the place. Then again, they would have posed like that even if they were simply friends and nothing more.

Who knew what other pictures of them had been captured—the press was everywhere at this event, dubbed the most photographed event in the world. And not just the media, but amateur photographers probably made up a huge portion of the crowd of half a million or more people, most of them competing for best photograph.

"We don't have time for this," Kyle whispered in her ear.

Fortunately the photographer moved on to another balloon.

Kyle flamed the propane burner again, and Nikki felt the basket shift, but her crew held them tethered to the ground.

"We made it." He sighed.

"And you had any doubts?" she teased. It could take fifteen to twenty minutes to set up a balloon, but with such a huge volume competing, they had to be quick about it because they had to go up in groups. All the balloons couldn't go up at once. "It's not like this is our first event. We've already competed in too many, if you ask me."

And, in fact, this would be their last competition—the last day of the fiesta.

Kyle smiled at her but didn't respond. He was wound tight, as if he had something to prove, but also as if he loved every minute of this. Nikki struggled to look at him without seeing Jordan's smiling face right alongside him. But maybe that wasn't a bad thing, and maybe things would always be this way.

Unless, of course, she moved. Nikki forced the thought from her mind—she didn't want to think about that right now but would prefer to enjoy this time with Kyle. She might not get more than this, and if not, that would be her decision.

Mine alone.

Kyle loved her, and as she watched his taut muscles work through the competitions, and his adorable, grinning face, she almost floated on the love she had for him. And that terrified her.

When Jordan died, Kyle left without a word. Just disappeared from the face of the earth. There was no beating his chest and blaming him or crying against his shoulder. She didn't have the chance to reminisce with him about Jordan, to laugh and cry at the memories. He didn't even

attend the funeral. She couldn't help but think that someone who could do that could leave for any reason.

"Earth to Nikki," Kyle said, waving his hand in front
of her face. "We're lifting off."

Too caught up in her confusing thoughts, Nikki had
missed the signal. They drifted upward with the others
in the competition as the air in the envelope grew hotter.
From Fiesta Park they would travel toward the north part
for the Prize Ring Toss competition.

"So, which one of us is going to toss the ring?"

Kyle gave her a look. "Are you kidding me?"

"No, I'm not kidding."

"You couldn't hit the broad side of a barn with a Frisbee."
He chuckled, his playful gaze challenging her. "So far, your
efforts to drop the markers close to the target have been a
complete fail."

Most of the competitions they'd competed in were a
simple matter of dropping markers close to a target. They'd
competed in the Sid Cutter Memorial yesterday. Sid Cutter
was the founder of the Albuquerque International Balloon
Fiesta. Nikki's father told her the man had served in the
air force as a pilot and one day was helping a friend out
with a balloon when he ended up aloft without a pilot and
didn't know what he was doing. He had to figure things
out fast, but he fell in love with balloons then.

Nikki scowled, teasing, and accepting Kyle's challenging taunt. "That's partly pilot error. You couldn't get us
close enough for any amount of beanbag-tossing skills."

"I could have had a full house in the hold-'em-poker
competition. I had a great hand."

"Oh, now, you can't blame me for that one." She had
gotten as close as she could, but the slight gust of wind
and the next thing she knew, Kyle had dropped his markers on the wrong cards.

"I'm going to blame you for something if you don't stop distracting me. That blue and gold is going to collide with us if I don't get us higher."

Nikki sucked in a breath and watched as the balloon envelope pushed up against their basket, tilting it forward.

Kyle and Nikki fell against the side of the basket. He gripped her arm as if it was his job to protect her and gave the envelope a hefty dose of flaming propane.

"Hang on," he said.

As their own balloon went higher, their basket was freed from the other balloon and rocked back and forth. Nervous laughter escaped. "I forgot how that feels."

"Sorry about that."

"Hey, it's not your fault." Nikki squeezed his arm.

Kyle glanced at her, his gaze lingering, and searching a little longer than necessary. He returned his focus to their quickly approaching target.

"You've done great this week." Nikki leaned against the basket and enjoyed the view, including Kyle. She smiled to herself. "You're really good, you know. An expert pilot."

Jordan would be so proud of you. In fact, so would Dad.

"Thanks. You're not too shabby yourself." Kyle smiled, but his attention remained on his task.

She loved that about him—he wasn't easily distracted when he had a job to do.

"We both know that you're the better pilot. I'll admit it, okay? And while you might be better at getting us close to the pole, I don't think I can toss the ring, after all." For the Prize Ring Toss, they had to place a ring over the top of a thirty-foot pole.

"Okay. I'll get us in close and then you man the helm." He winked.

They drifted with the other competing balloons in silence until finally the pole came into view.

Kyle flipped the ring around in his hand.

Nikki wanted to tease that he took the competition way too seriously, but then again, a lot of prizes came with the wins, including a cash prize for this one.

Their balloon drifted forward, and Kyle readied himself to slip the ring over the pole. He'd done a great job of positioning their basket just right, but Nikki tensed all the same.

The pole was there, a few feet ahead, and Kyle leaned out of the basket, preparing to drop the ring.

The balloon seemed to drift too slowly. Too late, Nikki realized they were too far from the pole. Kyle leaned out of the basket.

"Be careful," she said.

He leaned even farther.

He wouldn't appreciate her distracting him, but she had to ask anyway. "What are you doing?"

"Getting closer. That's what."

Nikki couldn't help herself. She grabbed him—not to pull him back in but to make sure he didn't fall completely out.

And then…the pole was there.

Directly beneath them.

Kyle held the ring out just so.

He dropped it.

Nikki held her breath.

The ring slipped over the pole. The crowd erupted, and Kyle let out a whoop of his own as Nikki shouted her excitement. She threw her arms around the guy. Kyle squeezed her to him and slipped in a quick peck to her neck.

He released her as the balloon continued on with the wind. So far they'd been the only ones to place the ring.

"Too bad we won't know until later if we actually won something," she said.

"Of course we won something." Longing poured from his gaze.

Nikki couldn't look away. Kyle grinned as if he knew he'd pinned her in place. Cupping his palm against her cheek, he leaned in for a real kiss this time. Tender and sweet.

She was pretty sure he'd finally won her complete trust.
I love you, Kyle.

That evening, Kyle and Nikki agreed to meet up later at Pilots' Landing—a place for pilots to hang out, eat and share stories. They hadn't won any competitions, but they'd had fun. Music and voices filling his ears like those at a carnival, Kyle grabbed a drink at a concession stand and headed back to check on the balloon crew as they packed up, when a guy bumped into him, causing the soda and ice to slosh from his cup.

Kyle froze. No, it couldn't be.

Not yet, anyway.

He whirled.

Taylor Jenkins, his copilot in the upcoming Gordon Bennett stood looking back, too. In the end, they'd finally agreed that just the two of them would pilot the race.

"Thought I'd never find you in this crowd." The guy made his way to Kyle and wrapped his arm around his shoulders. "Good to see you, man."

"You, too," Kyle said, but he didn't mean a word of it. "What are you doing so far from home?" And so soon?

Stupid question, considering how many people from around the country and the world attended the event. But Kyle hadn't expected to see Jenkins. He wasn't supposed to be in town until next week, when they'd start preparing for the big race. Then again, next week started tomorrow. Idiot.

"What? You don't look happy to see me," he said.

"I'm surprised, that's all." Kyle searched the grounds, hoping Nikki wouldn't make an unexpected appearance, as well. Somehow, he had to lose Jenkins. Find Nikki and tell her everything before it was too late. Before someone else told her.

He'd kept hoping for the right time to break the news to her. There hadn't been one.

"You're surprised to see me at just the biggest ballooning event of the year?" Jenkins laughed.

"You're right. I'm an idiot. But you should have said something. How long have you been in town?" Kyle chugged some of his soda. Jenkins hadn't been able to take enough time off his job as a corporate executive to participate in the fiesta *and* the Gordon Bennett. Or so he'd said, and yet he was here.

"Got here a couple of days ago. A guy's gotta work. The reason I didn't contact you sooner is that I know you had your focus on this. I didn't want to distract you."

Kyle nodded, tension cording around his neck and shoulders. He needed an excuse to escape. He was supposed to meet Nikki, and he could *not* show up with Jenkins. Not until he'd talked to her first. But he couldn't be rude, either.

"So what's on for tonight?" Kyle asked. "Got any plans?"

"As a matter of fact, I have a hot date." Jenkins thrust his hand out. "It was good to run into you. Call me when you're done here and we can meet up. Hard to believe that only two weeks out and we'll have a chance to make a name for ourselves."

Kyle nodded, shaking his friend's hand.

"Yep, make a name for ourselves." His words sounded as hollow as they felt.

"See you later." Jenkins turned and walked away, disappearing into the crowd.

Kyle waited until he was a good distance in the opposite direction, chugging his soda until it was gone. He pressed his hands over his face, rubbing his eye sockets. Staring into the crowd, he called Nikki on her cell.

Come on, come on, come on. She didn't pick up. Could be for any number of reasons. Kyle couldn't steady his voice enough to leave a message. He pressed on to Pilots' Landing, their meeting place. As soon as he found her he'd have to tell her.

There was no more time.

A knot wrenched in his gut. Oddly enough, it was almost the hardest thing he would ever have to say.

Chapter 17

Kyle stepped into Pilots' Landing. The place was thick with enthusiasm. He spotted more award-winning balloon pilots in the group than he could count on both hands. Though there were female pilots aplenty, there were more men and lots of testosterone, stirred by days of competition.

Long tables were laden with everyday fare like burgers that he could top with cheese and green chilis if he wanted to eat New Mexico style, and chimichangas, burritos and more exotic Albuquerque cuisine. He'd been hungry moments before, but the news he had to tell Nikki had snuffed out his appetite. Instead, he passed up the tables and stood against the far wall, where he caught snippets of conversations here and there. If there was one thing he knew, it was that balloon pilots loved to share their tales. It was all about adventure.

He recalled Nikki's father telling his balloon stories, and for the first time he realized those stories had been what stirred the balloon fever inside him. It wasn't long before Jordan became like his father, and if Kyle was honest, he wasn't any different. Now that he thought about it, almost all his conversations with Michael were about his ballooning adventures.

But the stories were memories. Important memories. And that was what flying a balloon was all about, what life was all about—making memories. Good ones.

Of course, there were always exceptions. Kyle had his work cut out for him to erase the bad memories and his contributions. Held captive by his tumultuous thoughts, Kyle hadn't noticed when the conversations died down. Hart Baker was talking now. Baker was a man with a long list of ballooning accomplishments. Kyle caught the end of his spiel.

"This just goes to show how you can't let yourself get distracted. I don't even remember what caught my attention, but it wasn't where it should have been and the balloon dipped into the pond."

Laughter and groans abounded.

"Now, now, I was quick to get the balloon high, and water spilled from the basket, which was inspiring all by itself. The passengers were a little wet, but no worse for the wear."

"Talk about a soft landing," someone else said.

The group laughed and voices rose again. Kyle spotted Nikki across the large space and started to make his way over to her, when Baker said his name.

Kyle paused, thinking he must have misheard.

"Kyle Morgan," he said, this time leaving no doubt. "You have a story to tell. I don't think I'm alone in wanting to hear it."

The room resounded with collective agreement.

Really?

Kyle's gaze flicked to Nikki's and he held it—her blueberry eyes grew wide and pensive. She stood there waiting, expectant, just like everyone in the room. Did she want him to tell them a story he hadn't told her yet? He wasn't sure he even could. Sweat beaded at his temples.

He needed to make his way across the room right now and drag Nikki out of here and tell her about his one last promise.

Why had he made such an insane promise to Jordan?

Why was he trying to keep it now when it would only end up hurting the woman he loved? Seeing the expectant faces, he knew he had to keep that promise.

For Jordan.

And somehow, he had to make her understand.

He shoved the recent nightmares of his ordeal out of his mind before he ended up looking like a coward in front of these people. His peers. It had been three years. Surely he could talk about it now.

Then Jenkins stepped into the room.

Time's up.

How could he make it to Nikki and tell her before Jenkins caught up with him? But he had to try. Shifting on his feet, Kyle jammed his hands in his pockets and allowed his gaze to glance off several faces in the group of about two hundred. "Jordan Alexander was… He was my best friend in the world."

The words made him sound like a little kid. But that was when they'd met. Kyle smiled, thinking good thoughts about his friend. He tried to focus on the positive side to a story with a tragic ending. "There was nothing he enjoyed more than flying balloons. It was the family business, you know."

Again, he locked eyes with Nikki. She appeared captivated by his words. *Go on,* her eyes seemed to plead.

"When the chance came for us to compete in the Gordon Bennett, Jordan didn't hesitate. Neither did I." A few laughed, but they all knew what was coming next. "You sure you want to hear this?" His voice hitched with the question.

"If you're comfortable telling it," Hart said, "we want to hear your story. In a way, we're all in this together. Loving to fly and knowing the risks."

Murmurs of agreement resounded.

Kyle wasn't sure he was comfortable, and he couldn't imagine why they'd want to hear something that ended in tragedy. It would ruin everyone's mood, including his own. And the truth was, Jordan had hesitated but maybe for, like, a millisecond, especially with Kyle's overbearing insistence. That was why neither of them had listened to Nikki or her mother when they tried to talk Kyle and Jordan out of competing.

But Nikki said nothing now to correct him. She acted as if she expected him to keep talking, too.

He shifted on his feet, thinking about how to put his tale into words. *You can do this.* He allowed the images to take over. Instead of the group of balloon pilots watching him, he saw the gas balloon. He saw Jordan's face and the European countries below him. Then the Mediterranean.

A memory hit him and he laughed to himself, except everyone was watching. "Jordan has to be the greatest pilot I've ever known. No offense, Hart."

The man smiled. "None taken, son."

In a way, sharing about Jordan like this could be a memorial to him. Kyle knew it was the right thing to do. Let them see the man as the hero he was. "It takes someone brave and fearless to be the kind of single father he was. The kind of loving son and brother. The kind of friend he was to me.

"And he piloted his balloons in competitions with the same fearless attitude, though remaining aware and conscientious about safety, as well. We'd been in the air for three, going on four, days already when we saw the storm in the distance. We were over water, and both of us had that gut feeling that if we could stay in the air just a little longer we could actually win this thing. What more fitting than for us to win—two guys from Albuquerque, New Mexico, where the greatest ballooning event in the world takes place."

That comment elicited some whoops. Still, a good number of the pilots in the room weren't from the region. The thought of what came next tightened around his chest, squeezing. Kyle struggled to speak, the images playing across his mind.

"The storm—it came on us faster than we'd experienced before." They should have landed. Kyle urged Jordan to land, but he was too confident in his own abilities. His own invincibility. But this wasn't the place to lay any blame. "We were so close…"

Heavy expectation weighed across the room. "The wind caught us."

Kyle squeezed his eyes shut. They didn't want to hear this. Hart didn't know what he was asking. Or did he? It was like being on a ride in an amusement park, only one that had gone out of control. They were flung through the air like so much trash, and then the balloon had started deflating. Quickly. Seeing their chance, Kyle and Jordan had agreed to jump to the water below when they were close enough—it was a better choice than a hard landing on the approaching coast of Italy.

Kyle hit the water. But Jordan's foot had snagged.

I can't finish this.

"Jordan died doing what he loved." It was too hard—and

too private—to speak of those last moments with Jordan, when he'd made his way to shore and found the basket.

Tears streamed from Nikki's eyes—tears and love.

Kyle's heart pounded against his ribs. Now. He needed to tell her now, in front of all these people. He drew in a breath—

Someone squeezed his shoulder from behind. Jenkins. Didn't the guy have a hot date?

"And this guy is brave enough to go after the gold again."

Kyle glanced at Jenkins, at the smile plastering his face. Any words that might have come, Kyle choked on.

"In case you haven't heard yet, he's my copilot in the next Gordon Bennett."

The room erupted in cheers, congratulating them.

Jenkins pumped his fist in the air. "For Jordan!"

But Kyle's only thought was for Nikki.

She tore her pain-filled gaze from him and ran from the room.

Ignoring the congratulatory cheers for Kyle and his copilot, Nikki shoved through the door, nausea swirling in her stomach. She stepped out of the way and around the corner of the building, back into the shadows, and gripped her midsection. Her vision blurred with tears, the vibrant colors of balloons melded together, but this time they brought her no comfort.

Her breaths came deep and hard.

I have to keep it together. Make it to the minivan. Good thing they were done with the competitions—Nikki couldn't face Kyle anytime soon, if ever.

Clearing her vision, the rush of emotion that warred to be free, she shoved away from the wall, trying to ignore the resounding announcement that Kyle was competing in the Gordon Bennett. Pain slashed across her heart and left an open, inflamed wound.

After everything. How could he?

Focus. She had to focus on getting to the minivan. She picked up the pace, afraid her heart would explode in front of hundreds of people before she made it to the privacy of her vehicle. Then she wasn't sure how she'd make it home.

She bumped into someone. "Oh, sorry," she said.

"Watch it," he said. The voice sounded familiar, but Nikki couldn't see through her tears and kept moving.

Moments later, a hand gripped her arm and squeezed, whipping her around.

Through fluid vision, Nikki saw Kyle standing there. Her knees wanted to crumple, but she stood strong.

"Leave me alone." Nikki turned and walked away and then started to jog.

"Nikki!" Kyle called.

She didn't care. She could not face him now with everyone watching. She didn't know if she could ever look at him again the same way.

He stood in front of her, blocking her way, and gripped both arms. "Nikki, listen to me. Give me a chance."

His words were breathy, his expression distraught.

"You had your chance, Kyle." Nikki covered her eyes. She so didn't want to cry.

Drawing in a breath, she held her tears inside and gave way to fury and hurt. "After everything you've put my family through, after the tirade you threw about me flying in the American Challenge, that you could go and do this, I just can't believe it. And you *kept* it from me this whole time."

"And this is why. Because of the way you're acting now. How could I tell you that Jordan made me promise to compete again? To win for him." Kyle released her and dropped his hands to his sides. "To win for him, Nikki. Do you really think I wanted to hurt you?"

"You could have told me...." Her voice broke a whisper. "And to go and use Jordan like that, telling all those people you're going to win the race for him. How dare you?" Nikki shoved by him, her fury and hurt melding into a solid anvil of resentment.

Kyle kept pace with her. "I didn't do that. I didn't say it was for Jordan. Jenkins said it. I was looking for you and planned to tell you tonight. I had no idea—"

"Save it." Nikki could see the parking lot ahead of her. "It doesn't matter now."

"How can you say that?"

Nikki huffed and trudged forward, hoping Kyle would give up. But he stood in front of her again, wanting her attention.

"I should have told you, all right? Give a guy a break. I'm sorry. Can you please forgive me?"

There was that word again. *Forgive.* She wanted to ask him how many times she would have to forgive him, but she knew the Lord's answer to that. "That will take me some time, Kyle, but it doesn't mean I can watch you race in the Gordon Bennett. Doesn't mean I want to sit around and wait for you to show up. I...I can't trust you. Count on you."

Now the tears were threatening again.

"You can't think this is the same situation as when I left. Those were completely different circumstances and reasons. But I promise, I won't make the same mistake I made before, Nikki. I'm going to win this race, and then I'm coming back for you and Michael."

He said it with such desperate hope, but the words pressed against her fresh wound. The tears streamed down her cheeks freely now. Except they weren't tears of joy.

"There's no need. I'm taking that job in Tulsa. I have an offer on the business. If there's one thing you should have learned through all this it's never to make promises. Keeping them is too hard. But here's another one for you, since you're so bent on keeping them at all costs—promise never to speak to me again."

Kyle stepped back as if she had slapped him, only her words had hurt worse than her striking him ever could.

This was wrong. All wrong. Didn't she love this man? And that was why it hurt all the more. She took his stunned reaction as her chance and stepped by him, making a beeline for the parking lot.

This time, she had no doubt that Kyle wouldn't follow.

Chapter 18

The sting of Nikki's words kept him from moving. His heart lay filleted, Nikki style, behind his ribs.

She didn't really mean them...

A knot twisted in Kyle's throat. He wasn't sure she didn't.

Kyle watched her walk away from him, knowing that even if he could move, following her was useless. He would never convince her of anything until she'd had time to process the news. News she believed was nothing but betrayal on Kyle's part.

He only had himself to blame. What was new?

I should have told her when I had the chance.

Scraping his hands through his hair, he watched her disappearing into the crowd. Why was it so hard to do the right thing, keep promises and protect those you loved? So far, that strategy never worked out for him. Couldn't Nikki see that he hadn't meant to hurt her? He'd only meant to keep his promise? Why couldn't she understand that he feared her reaction, and that was why he'd wanted to tell her at the right time?

How had everything blown out of control like that? He'd known when he'd seen Jenkins that he was heading for a hard landing.

In the distance, Nikki almost looked as if she was jogging. To get away from him faster, no doubt.

He wanted to turn and run away, too. He couldn't stand to watch the woman he loved walk away from him like this. At the moment, he knew she meant the promise she'd wanted to extract from him. He hadn't given it. Had she noticed that? He could only hope her feelings of betrayal, hurt and anger would fade with the light of understanding.

God, please, help her. Help me. And poor Michael.

Coming back to New Mexico had seemed like the right thing and the right time. But now he saw he'd only hurt Nikki and her family all over again. And if he stayed away, never speaking to her again, he'd only prove her right— that she couldn't count on him. But he didn't plan to make that same mistake twice—he wasn't going to disappear this time, not so easily.

Someone shoved away from the side of a building and followed a few yards behind Nikki. Kyle had never met Nathan and had only seen a picture of him with one of the balloons. It hung on the wall back at Sky High. But Kyle was pretty sure that was him.

Why was Nathan following her? Kyle had every intention of finding out, and maybe there was plenty about this situation that he couldn't fix, but at least he might have a chance to take care of one thing before he left for France and the Gordon Bennett.

Kyle made to follow Nathan. Demanding answers from the guy wouldn't produce anything. The police had already tried that. He hadn't been charged, and they were beyond busy with a million extra people in the city this week.

Nathan would have to be caught in the act, whatever that might be. Kyle glanced behind him, taking a good long look at Fiesta Park. He doubted this would be the last time he was there, but it might be the last time he was there with Nikki or the Sky High team.

Nikki headed straight for her minivan, and Kyle hung back a little, knowing she would probably glance up. He thought it was better if she didn't spot him following. He stepped behind a balloon trailer, keeping his eye on Nathan, who'd also apparently parked his vehicle in the lot meant for balloon pilots. As far as he knew, Nathan hadn't competed. But there were hundreds of balloons. How could he know unless he read the list of pilots, which he hadn't?

Though he knew Nikki wouldn't take his call, he needed to warn her about Nathan. He left a voice mail instructing her to look out for Nathan, who appeared to be following her. He texted her, too. She might delete his voice mail without listening, but maybe something in his text would catch her attention.

In the meantime, he'd follow Nathan. He had to hoof it in order to reach his Denali and catch up to them in this traffic. Nikki inched into the cars jammed on the street, trying to exit the park, Nathan a few cars behind her. Kyle a couple of cars behind him. This wasn't going to work. She was going to see Kyle, for one thing, if she dared to pay any attention, but she was probably still too upset.

He doubted he could follow Nathan in the thick traffic, either. But he could guess that Nikki was headed home, so if he lost her, he'd make sure that she made it there without incident. Make sure that Nathan wasn't in the neighborhood.

His cell rang.

Mark.

Kyle could only imagine the colorful words Mark might have for him. Kyle answered the call via the Bluetooth speakers.

Mark let him have it. Just as if he was Nikki's father bent on watching out for his little girl. Gritting his teeth, Kyle let the man have his say. How had he found out so fast? Had Nikki told him what she'd learned?

"What do you have to say for yourself?" Mark asked.

So *now* he wanted to listen to Kyle's side of the story, part of which the man already knew and understood. But the guy had a soft heart where Nikki was concerned.

Kyle wanted to bring up that Mark could have told her himself, but he refrained for now. "We might have bigger problems, Mark. I'm following Nathan right now. He's following Nikki. I tried to call and text her, but she's not answering. Can you get through?"

Silence filled the Denali.

"I'll tell her. What are you going to do?"

"I'm going to follow her until I know she's safe. I'd like to follow Nathan to see if he does anything. I don't think it's my imagination that he's following her. And it's just too weird to be a coincidence."

"I think you're right. You follow Nathan. I'll make sure that Nikki arrives home safely. I'll check on her."

Promise? No. Kyle was done with asking for them. Done with giving them, for a while, at least. He could trust Mark without extracting a guarantee from him.

A weighty sigh filled the cab of the Denali. "Listen, Kyle, I'm sorry about what I said. I'm just upset. I don't like to see Nikki get hurt. Maybe you could have handled the issue better or differently, but it's a tough situation no matter how you look at it. She would have reacted like this no matter when you told her, I'm guessing."

"Yeah. Maybe. I appreciate that. But how did she react when you told her that you knew I would compete?"

"That's why I understand your struggle—I have the same one. But I'll tell her when I get to her house tonight."

"Yeah, well, she might have something to tell you, too. I don't know if she meant the words or not, but she said she's taking the job and she has an offer on the business."

Another sigh. "It was my job to help her with that. I knew that was coming and so did you. But one day at a time. Let's make it through this day. Tomorrow brings enough troubles of its own."

Kyle and Mark ended the call. Nikki and Nathan got on the freeway, but Nathan exited. He wasn't following Nikki now, after all. Maybe he'd spotted Kyle's Denali, but he followed the guy anyway.

What are you planning, Nathan?

When Nathan pulled through the drive-through of a fast-food restaurant, Kyle decided to let him go. This could take all night. Mark had Nikki covered. Kyle would watch the warehouse tonight, especially since the restaurant Nathan had chosen to visit was only a couple of blocks away. If he decided to hit the warehouse tonight, Kyle would be there and waiting.

If what Nikki said was true, the problem wouldn't be theirs for much longer. The vandalism would belong to the next owner, but somehow, Kyle had a feeling it wouldn't transfer to the person who planned to buy the business.

Nikki didn't want to see him right now, and he had to admit, she might never want to see him again, just as she claimed. He wanted to be at the warehouse to think through his decisions. To get one last look at it, just in case.

Nikki couldn't go home yet. She couldn't face Mom or let Michael see her distress. He would instantly know something was wrong. Nor was she about to take any calls from Kyle or even Mark. They both already knew something was wrong, but she couldn't talk about it yet.

She needed to be alone. Get her head and heart together first. She turned around and headed to the warehouse. Chase was keeping their one and only balloon and trailer at his house the past couple of weeks until they got a handle on the vandalism. The warehouse would be empty tonight—no doubt there. The person intent on causing her grief, wreaking havoc on her business, only did so late at night, when the warehouse was empty. He or she had been careful to hide their identity. There'd never been a reason to be afraid of going there, and she wasn't about to start now.

She pulled into the parking lot and climbed from the minivan. The sky had grown dark already when Nikki unlocked the door and flipped on the lights inside.

Her footsteps echoed in the quiet building that had housed her father's business for so long. Realization finally slammed into her. Sky High would no longer be hers once the paperwork went through. A huge sense of loss engulfed her.

Not just for the warehouse but for Kyle.

Here, all alone at the business her father had built, she could release her pent-up frustrations. The racking sobs came now, and, leaning against the wall, Nikki slid to the floor.

This week had been one of the happiest in her life—the time she'd spent with Kyle had been everything she'd dreamed, except for that one dark moment in their history. A dark moment that overshadowed everything in her relationship with him.

Even if she ignored it, it wouldn't go away. She'd forgiven, but it didn't seem to matter. Her heart was broken all over again. She wished, oh, how she wished, she could see things the way Kyle saw them—that competing again for Jordan was a good thing.

She just couldn't let go of feeling as if he'd betrayed her. Kept something so important from her. Shouldn't that decision, of *all* decisions, have been something he talked about with her, especially if he was thinking of them in terms of having a future together? Especially since he'd told her that he loved her.

She had to think of more than herself. She had to think of Michael.

"Oh, Kyle, why did you make me love you?"

In the dark hidden corner behind a few shelves and junk where Kyle could remain well hidden, he covered his eyes, his shoulders shaking. When he'd heard someone coming in, he thought to hide, hoping to catch Nathan in an act of vandalism. Catch it all on video.

But Nikki had flipped on the lights that illuminated only a small portion of the warehouse. She'd been the one to step from the shadows, and Kyle had frozen.

Panicked, more like. She didn't want to see him here. He'd parked at McDonald's across the street and walked over so Nathan would think the place was empty.

When she'd broken into sobs and dropped to the floor, Kyle had taken a single step, aware that he needed to make his presence known. But he'd hesitated. He wasn't supposed to see this. She would be angry if he appeared now, and she'd be angry if he waited and watched.

What should he do?

Her pain resounded in her sobs and ripped through him like a tempest, carrying him forward on her grief—he felt it acutely, as if it were his own. And it was—he loved her.

I did this to her...

Chapter 19

Nikki shuddered, feeling the last of the torrent finally dissipate—a torrent that she'd held dammed inside for three years. She'd never allowed herself to fully grieve for Jordan, believing she needed to stay strong for Michael and for Mom.

Coming full circle and watching Kyle enter that race again, the fact that this time she'd sent him away and asked him never to return, had demolished that dam. Her eyes felt swollen and her nose was a mess.

A sound drew her attention, and she glanced around the warehouse. She *was* alone, wasn't she?

Nathan stepped from the shadows of the doorway.

Nikki's breath caught in her throat. Seconds ticked by before she could respond. She wanted to ask him how he'd gotten in since she'd locked the door behind her, but she already knew. The police had told Mark that someone who knew what they were doing and wanted to get inside could get in however they needed to get in, and even disconnect alarm systems, though she hadn't turned it on when she'd come inside.

Idiot. She needed to act as if everything was normal. *Don't give him the idea that you're scared or you suspect him.* She got to her feet.

"Nathan. Can I help you?"

"You want to help me? After you fired me?"

Nikki pressed against the wall. There wasn't anywhere for her to go. "Nathan…that was over two years ago. Why are you still holding on to that?"

"You're right, of course. I shouldn't hold a grudge."

Nikki frowned. She held her palms out. "Look, I'm sorry I fired you. Frankly, you made a mess of the schedule too many times. I couldn't afford the mistakes. I had to let you go."

Something flashed and Nikki looked down to see a knife. Fear tried to strangle her, but she was tired of being the victim and something rose up inside. "Did you come here planning to slash another balloon or tires?"

Then she remembered. Her minivan was parked out front. He had to know she was in here. He hadn't come for balloons or tires this time.

"No." He grinned. "I thought we could talk."

Her mouth dry, Nikki tried to hide that she was getting spooked. "I'm listening."

"Let's take a balloon up. I've always wanted to do that with you."

He was insane. What would Nathan do when he heard the news? "The one working balloon isn't here. We keep it somewhere else for now."

"So it would be safe, I guess." He laughed and crept closer. "That's too bad. Makes it hard to sell your business with only one, doesn't it?"

Though he didn't brandish the knife, Nikki knew it was

there all the same. Her breaths came hard and fast again. Nathan had to sense her panic.

Her selling had been the factor that put Sky High back on his radar, it seemed. "About the business. Are you interested in buying? How about if I sell it to you for half of what I was asking?" Or give it to him. Whatever it took to get away.

Keep him talking until someone came to the warehouse. Not likely.

Lord, a little help here, please?

If she hadn't told Kyle she never wanted to see him again, none of this would have happened. She'd be with him right now. Now there was no chance he would come back here, after the things she'd said.

"I get the feeling you'll forget you made the offer in the morning."

Nikki nearly gasped when she saw Kyle behind Nathan but quickly recovered, careful not to change her expression or telegraph his presence. "I can put something in writing right here and now."

"You'd...do that?" Nathan's eyes softened.

Remorse spilled into Nikki's thoughts—Nathan believed her. And she'd wanted that, hadn't she? And yet...

"I can see that you're lying."

"You're holding a knife. You've been vandalizing my property. Stole my balloon. Why would you believe I'd sell to you if I weren't under duress?"

Nathan growled. Before he could step closer, Kyle yanked him around and slammed his fist into the guy's face. The punch sent Nathan backward, but he didn't fall. Instead, he lashed out with the knife. Nikki slipped out of the way and into the office. All Kyle needed was for Nathan to grab her and hold a knife to her throat. While she watched through the glass, she called the police.

He lashed across Kyle's chest, drawing blood. But Kyle grabbed his wrist and twisted the knife out of his hand, then he punched him again. This time, Nathan fell to the floor and didn't get up.

Kyle ran his hand over his injury and drew it back to examine the blood. Nikki ran to him but came up short.

He looked at her. "Call the police?"

She nodded. "Already done. Are you...are you all right?"

"Just a flesh wound. Doesn't hurt in comparison to other wounds."

Nikki knew what he meant. Felt it to her bones. "I'm so glad you showed up when you did."

She couldn't help herself. Old habits died hard. Nikki took a step closer, wanting to rush into his arms. Needing to rush into his arms. But Kyle was a bronze statue, cold and unfeeling. She'd told him she never wanted him to speak to her again. Was that why he was being so distant?

"I've been here the whole time."

"You wha...?"

He slowly nodded. "I wanted to catch Nathan in the act. If you had listened to your voice mails, answered your calls or texts, you would have known he was following you. I was waiting here on the hunch he might show up tonight. You showed up first."

Heat flamed her cheeks. "Then you saw me.... Why didn't you say something?"

"You took me by surprise. I was too weighed with the emotion coming off you to move, and when I started, Nathan showed up. He was so close to you, I wanted to reach him before he could get to you first. If I let on that I was here, too, he might have grabbed you. Do you understand?"

Nikki thought back to the flood of tears. She'd thought she was all alone and had the freedom to let everything go. She wished Kyle hadn't seen that, but she understood and nodded.

"Apparently, Nathan was holding on to a longtime grudge." Kyle studied her, indictment in his eyes.

"I'm not holding on to a grudge, Kyle. I forgave you. I told you that, but it's not about that. I can't count on you."

Hurt flashed across his face, and he glanced down at Nathan, who was still on the floor. "You can't?"

Granted, he'd been here for her at this moment.

Sirens rang out in the distance, growing louder, and pressing Nikki. If she had anything to say, she'd better say it now. The tension between them was almost unbearable.

"I can't watch you compete in the Gordon Bennett, Kyle. I need *you* to understand. And as for everything else, you hurt me tonight. It's going to take some time."

"You're not the only one who is hurt. If I could take it all back, I would. At least I could take care of this—" he gestured at Nathan "—before I left."

Someone banged on the door, and Nikki ran to let the police in. An EMT followed soon after and examined both Nathan and Kyle. Kyle refused to go to the hospital but insisted on being treated in the ambulance while it idled in the parking lot for what he claimed was a flesh wound.

Nathan was handcuffed and stuffed into the backseat of a cruiser.

After Nikki gave her statement, she looked for Kyle, but he was gone. Mark was there, though, and opened his arms. She rushed to him, pressing her face into his shoulder.

"I came to say goodbye." Kyle's voice startled her. She pulled from Mark's fatherly embrace to look at Kyle.

"Goodbye?"

"Yes. I have to prepare for the Gordon Bennett. I have a friend that I'll send by next week. He's a great pilot and is willing to take my place here and help Chase until you sell the business. If you need him, that is."

Kyle's wry grin was superficial.

So it was over, then. All because of Kyle's mistake and Nikki's inability to let it go. Pathetic. "What about Michael? Can you at least—"

"I'll stop by and see him before I go. Don't worry. After that, I understand what you want from me." Kyle nodded, and even saluted, then turned his back on them and headed across the street to his vehicle.

Mark eyed her, a question in his gaze.

She knew what she'd asked of him, but in her deepest heart, she hoped and prayed this wasn't the last time she saw or heard from Kyle Morgan.

"I know what I said, Mom, but I have to watch this." Nikki held Michael on her lap as they looked at the Gordon Bennett tracking system on the computer. They'd been at it two days already.

Every so often, she'd stop packing long enough to look. Upon accepting Jeff's job offer, she'd traveled to Tulsa to find an apartment where they could live until they found a more permanent residence. She wanted to live in the area long enough before she decided where to either rent or purchase a home. Jeff had recommended the best school for Michael to attend, and she'd enroll him as soon as they moved in next week.

She was leaving behind the only home and life she'd ever known. Mom and Michael were, too.

"Look, there he is." Michael pointed at the live tracking marker indicating Kyle's balloon on the computer screen over Italy.

She and Michael had watched Kyle and Jenkins's balloon as well as the others since the race started. She prayed for his safety daily. In fact, every time she thought about him, which was almost continually.

Selling the business and getting a job far away had all been part of her plan for weeks. Months, even. But Kyle had showed up and turned everything sideways. Her plans—hopes and dreams—were coming to fruition, but she was beginning to have major doubts. Queasiness settled in her stomach every time she packed another box. She would miss the life she had here.

She was supposed to list Mom's house with a rental management company, but she'd held off doing that just yet. "Come on, sweetie. Time for bed."

Michael had stayed up later than usual because it was a Friday night, but Nikki finally insisted he get some rest. After settling Michael in bed, Nikki worked late into the night, though she hated packing. Maybe it was just an excuse so she could stay up and watch Kyle's progress across the Adriatic Sea now. Pray for his safety.

She shoved aside the angst that filled her every time she remembered the moment when Jordan and Kyle's balloon had disappeared. She'd seen the storm coming just like the rest of the world. Known it was probably a factor.

But not this time. She held on to hope, and so far the skies were clear. Growing tired and knowing she'd better rest if she wanted to keep up with Michael the next day, Nikki propped herself on a pillow on the sofa and set the laptop on her stomach, where she could watch.

When she opened her eyes, daylight streamed through the windows. Sometime in the night, Nikki had set her laptop on the coffee table—or had that been her mother? Regardless, she picked it up and retrieved the page to see Kyle's progress.

She gasped at the news banner crawling across the

page—the winners of the Gordon Bennett—Kyle Morgan and Taylor Jenkins.

Nikki jumped up and screamed, almost dropping the laptop. She ran through the house yelling the news for her mother and Michael to hear. Michael ran to her, and she wrapped him in her arms, swinging him around.

He pressed his hands against her cheeks. "Uncle Kyle won!"

"Yes, Sheriff Michael. Let me show you." Nikki sat Michael next to her on the sofa and stirred her laptop to life again. The banner scrolled across the screen, but there she found a streaming video of Kyle and Jenkins.

Kyle appeared exhausted, but it was Kyle—the man she loved. The man she'd sent away.

He lifted the Gordon Bennett cup. "I want to dedicate this to my best friend, Jordan Alexander, who lost his life three years ago when our balloon collapsed, and to his sister, the woman I love, Nikki Alexander."

Nikki cupped her hands over her face, tears streaming from her eyes as she watched. She couldn't believe he'd said those words for the entire world to hear.

"Is Uncle Kyle coming back, Mommy?"

Nikki was afraid to answer Michael. He wouldn't be happy living in Tulsa. He wouldn't be happy unless he could fly.

"I don't know, Sheriff. I don't know."

Chapter 20

A week after winning the race of a lifetime, a week after being declared one of the greatest balloon pilots in the world, Kyle had made all the media rounds he could stand to make before he parted ways with Jenkins, for the time being anyway, considering they had other business, and made his way in search of Nikki.

He learned from Mark that she and her mother had just moved into an apartment in Tulsa and were probably still unpacking. He wished that he could have somehow kept her from taking that step.

The fact that she'd taken it sent doubt crawling through him. Hadn't she said she didn't want to hear from him again? Hadn't he told himself he wouldn't interrupt her life in Tulsa unless she wanted him there?

Kyle had a lot of things to make up for and he had no guarantees that Nikki would let him, but he wasn't one to shy away from danger, or worse, the risk to his heart. As far as that went, his heart still lay shattered, pieces jumbling around in his rib cage every step he took.

But that hadn't stopped him from trying. He wasn't a quitter, and those three years he'd disappeared didn't count, considering he'd stepped back into the game. Eventually. And so he found himself standing in the breezeway of an apartment building, his hand poised to knock.

His other hand holding a bouquet of flowers—this time, fifty red roses. The little black velvet box holding the solitaire-diamond ring was burning a hole in his pocket, as if he'd kept the propane valve open too long.

Risky business, this, but he wouldn't have it any other way.

Kyle knocked, feeling the shock of fear as he'd never known, even when he'd plummeted hundreds of feet to the water that fateful day three years ago.

He sensed when someone looked through the peephole, and he drew in a calming breath. He had no idea what to expect and didn't have the right to expect anything at all except maybe a kick in the backside.

The door swung open, and Nikki stood there, her smile enough to send him flying, and while he soared on that confidence, he thrust the roses out. "These are for you."

She took them and tipped them toward her face, breathing in the scent. "Thank you. They're beautiful. Won't you come in?" She opened the door wide.

"Um, I'd love to, but could we…talk first?"

Nikki seemed to understand. Her smile warmed, and she turned to her mother. "Can you stick these in water? I'll be right back."

When Nikki stepped out, she shut the door behind her and jammed her hands into her slender jeans. Wow, he'd missed her. "Michael should be home soon. He's playing with a new friend just a few doors down. He'll be glad to see you."

Tension emanated from Nikki, but not the bad kind. Of all the things he'd expected to see in her eyes and in her demeanor, he hadn't expected or deserved what he saw now. He'd barely opened his arms when she slipped into them. He savored her warmth and tenderness against him.

Brushed his fingers through her hair, drew in her lavender scent. "Oh, Nikki..."

Kyle eased back enough to inch his face near hers. When her chin edged up, that was all the encouragement he needed. Kyle pressed his lips against hers. All this, and he hadn't even proposed. Surely, she still loved him. Kyle eased out of the kiss but kept his face close.

"Nikki, I love you. I'm willing to give up hot-air balloons if that's what you want. Will you marry me?"

She sighed, her peppermint breath comforting. "I'm so sorry about everything that happened. Everything I said. You know I didn't mean it, right?"

"I think so, yes. I guess by your reaction, I hope so. But, Nikki, did you hear me? I just proposed."

"I know. I know. I just had to get that out. Yes, Kyle, I heard you, but I don't think you'll be happy if you're not floating around in the sky."

Her words sucked the oxygen from his lungs. Was she turning him down?

"No, Nikki. You're wrong. I won't be happy without you. It's all about you, and always has been. I realized that this time when I was drifting over France and Spain. The Mediterranean really drove it home for me. All I could think about was your eyes. I couldn't wait to get back to you." He grinned. "I realized that my joy and love of balloons is because you were there with me during all those times. And without you, there isn't any joy in it. There's no joy in anything. Please believe me—you're all I want."

Moisture flooded her gaze. "Oh, Kyle. You've made me happier than I ever dreamed. Yes, I'll marry you."

Kyle kissed her again but sensed something wasn't right. He gently squeezed her shoulders. "What's wrong?"

"I wish I hadn't sold the business. Wish we hadn't moved. I miss it already."

He smiled. "If you really mean that, I have something for you. I kind of thought you might feel that way, and though it was a risky move on my part, depending on what you said today, I had planned to give it to you as a wedding gift."

"What is it?"

"Please don't think me presumptuous."

"I wouldn't change anything about you, Kyle Morgan, presumptuous or otherwise."

"Jenkins bought Sky High through one of his businesses. He paid cash, so that's why it went through so fast. You probably didn't even know he was the buyer."

"What?"

"He agreed to sell it back to you if you want it. Reverse the sale, in essence."

"How did you talk him into that?"

"We had a lot of time to talk while we were drifting over Europe, remember? After hearing my story, he told me that if we won, he'd sell it back to you, to us, if we wanted. He knew I planned to propose. I think he was so enticed with the prospect of winning, he thought I could somehow make that happen, try a little harder, if I thought I could get your business back." Kyle sensed Nikki's overactive mind formulating an accusation. "But this is only if you want it, Nikki. No pressure. I just thought if you had any regrets, and if you agreed to marry me, what a better wedding gift. I couldn't stand to see your sad face, couldn't wait to tell you."

"Uncle Kyle, Uncle Kyle." Michael came running through the breezeway and wrapped his arms around Kyle's waist. "I'm so glad you're back and you're a winner!"

Kyle lifted Michael in his arms and squeezed Nikki to him. "Yeah, little buddy, I'm a winner. We're all winners."

"You can call me Captain Michael."

Oh, so it was Captain now.

"Okay, Captain Michael. Look what I got for your mommy?" In his excitement in seeing Nikki, and then in giving her his wedding gift before the fact, he'd forgotten the ring. He slipped it from his pocket now and popped open the box one-handed.

Nikki covered her face. Dropping her hands, she said, "It's beautiful!"

She reached for the ring, but Kyle held it out of her reach. He set Michael on his feet and took the ring out then dropped to one knee and cleared his throat. "Let me start over and do this the right way. Nikki Alexander, will you marry me?"

"Yes!"

Her mother opened the door at that moment to see Kyle on his knees, holding out the ring.

Epilogue

Six months later

Nikki in her gorgeous wedding dress and Kyle in his tux, they climbed into the gondola. *Intrepid,* Jordan's repaired hot-air balloon, floated eagerly above them, waiting to carry them on their very own wedding sunset balloon ride.

They waved at family and friends. Mark stood next to Mom, who held on to Michael. Thank goodness he seemed to understand this was a special time for Nikki and Uncle Kyle, who'd already stepped in to fill Jordan's shoes as Michael's father.

Nikki felt Kyle's hand slip around her waist and pull her close. He squeezed the lever and sent flames into the envelope, encouraging it to lift them higher and higher. Since they were both pilots, and Kyle had been recently dubbed one of the best pilots in the world, they'd agreed to take this flight alone.

The balloon drifting forward and leaving loved ones behind, Kyle leaned in for a long thorough kiss.

Nikki languished in it but soon shoved him away. "Pay attention to what you're doing here."

"I can multitask, Mrs. Morgan." Kyle feigned hurt but then winked.

His gaze brimmed with expectation and sent Nikki's pulse racing. She tore her eyes from him to watch the sunset. Intertwining her fingers with his, she sighed. "Isn't it beautiful, Kyle?"

"Just the first of many a sunrise and sunset we'll see together," he said, and then he drew her back into his arms.

* * * * *

REQUEST YOUR FREE BOOKS!

2 FREE CHRISTIAN NOVELS
PLUS 2
FREE
MYSTERY GIFTS

HEARTSONG
PRESENTS

YES! Please send me 2 Free Heartsong Presents novels and my 2 FREE mystery gifts (gifts are worth about $10). After receiving them, if I don't wish to receive any more books I can return the shipping statement marked "cancel." If I don't cancel, I will receive 4 brand-new novels every month and be billed just $4.24 per book in the U.S. and $5.24 per book in Canada. That's a savings of at least 20% off the cover price. It's quite a bargain! Shipping and handling is just 50¢ per book in the U.S. and 75¢ per book in Canada.* I understand that accepting the 2 free books and gifts places me under no obligation to buy anything. I can always return a shipment and cancel at any time. Even if I never buy another book, the two free books and gifts are mine to keep forever.

159/359 HDN FVYK

Name	(PLEASE PRINT)	
Address		Apt. #
City	State	Zip

Signature (if under 18, a parent or guardian must sign)

Mail to the Harlequin® Reader Service:
IN U.S.A.: P.O. Box 1867, Buffalo, NY 14240-1867

* Terms and prices subject to change without notice. Prices do not include applicable taxes. Sales tax applicable in N.Y. This offer is limited to one order per household. Not valid for current subscribers to Heartsong Presents books. All orders subject to credit approval. Credit or debit balances in a customer's account(s) may be offset by any other outstanding balance owed by or to the customer. Please allow 4 to 6 weeks for delivery. Offer available while quantities last. Offer valid only in the U.S.

Your Privacy—The Harlequin® Reader Service is committed to protecting your privacy. Our Privacy Policy is available online at www.ReaderService.com or upon request from the Harlequin Reader Service.
We make a portion of our mailing list available to reputable third parties that offer products we believe may interest you. If you prefer that we not exchange your name with third parties, or if you wish to clarify or modify your communication preferences, please visit us at www.ReaderService.com/consumerchoice or write to us at Harlequin Reader Service Preference Service, P.O. Box 9062, Buffalo, NY 14269. Include your complete name and address.

HSPDIR13R

HEARTSONG

PRESENTS

**Look out for 4 new
Heartsong Presents books next month!**

**Every month 4 inspiring faith-filled
romances will be available in stores.**

These contemporary and historical Christian
romances emphasize God's role in every
relationship and reinforce the importance of
faith, hope and love.

LIHP48648